BIG PULP

2016 Annual

Also by Bill Olver (editor)

Clones, Fairies & Monsters in the Closet (2013)
APESHIT (2013)
The Kennedy Curse (2013)
Black Chaos: Tales of the Zombie (2014)
Black Chaos II: More Tales of the Zombie (2015)
Way Out West (2015)

Other periodicals from Big Pulp Publications

Child of Words (SF&F)
M (horror & mystery)
Thirst (romance)

BIG PULP
2016 Annual

Science Fiction & Fantasy,
Horror, Mystery & Romance

Edited by
BILL OLVER

Big Pulp Publications

Credits

Big Pulp 2016 Annual

ISBN 978-0-9896812-4-7

Visit us online:
www.bigpulp.com
Facebook (Facebook.com/bigpulp)
Twitter (twitter.com/BigPulp)
Patreon (patreon.com/bigpulp)

Distributed by Ingram Periodicals.

Ebook versions available from Amazon and other online venues

Big Pulp Publications
BILL OLVER Editor/Publisher

Published by Big Pulp Publications
116 Greene Street Cumberland, MD 21502

Cover photo: "Monument to Yuri Gagarin" by Alexander Kuzovlev, photographer (Tattoo artist, Anton "Antonius" Ivkin)

Photographer, Alexander Kuzovlev http://onephotographer.ru/
Tattoo artist, Anton "Antonius" Ivkin: http://www.laborum.ru/antonius/

Table of Contents

ROMANCE

SCIENCE FICTION

Melancholy Dust

by JASON S. RIDLER

DEREK PEELED A THICK SLICE OF SKIN FROM HIS lip as he rifled through the banker-box on the cash desk that crushed his current guilty pleasure, the last story in Byron Priess's *Weird Heroes, Vol. 1*.

"The library said I couldn't give them all of his junk, can you believe that?" said the worm-lipped old woman. "Is that trash worth anything?"

Five minutes to closing, but he didn't care. Derek smiled, said "We'll see," and then breathed in the scent. "The loneliest smell in the world is a dusty book." He'd thought so the first shift he'd taken at Edelweiss Books. The heavy, depressing aroma had only grown in time until it deadened his sense of smell permanently. The scent of melancholy dust from every unwanted book was as unique as it was sad. He'd miss it.

Itches prickled his nose. He tossed aside the Zane Greys, covers as ragged as the lawmen dashing across them, another deep breath and the itch eased. "Huh. The Shadow. Neat."

"Goodness!" she said, covering her mouth. "I hated that radio show. I'll tell you what evil lurks in the heart of men." Her tone jabbed a memory out of its hiding space. A Salvation Army truck pulling out of the driveway, an empty closet, his comics gone; he'd run, but they caught him.

"Stop wiggling, Derek! We don't need fascist power fantasies sitting in my home."

"Too late, Mommy! He's already retarded."

"Emily! Don't say that!"

"She's right, Mother. Did you see his report card? Jane Morrison says he'll have to take the fifth grade again. Ow! Mom! He hit me! You saw it!"

"Let me go! Just let me go!"

"How much?" she said.

Derek sniffed. "Pulp novels aren't rare, yet…Wow! Walter Gibson signed it."

"Who?"

Derek traced the signature, enjoying the rough, acidic texture. Gibson, a friend of Houdini, a pulp writing machine, whose life was known and treasured by the fringe world of collectors and hobbyists. A rare treasure. Fitting for a last day.

"Look, I don't care if Moses wrote it on a napkin. Just tell me is it worth something?"

Mr. Fletcher had one rule with customers: fleece them dry. But it was his last day. "How does five hundred bucks sound?"

She wouldn't stop chatting as he got all the money from the reserve box under the cash. "How about the others? More gems?"

One minute to closing. He shrugged. "Let's see."

"Here, let me help you."

The box dropped, and a worn issue of *Hustler* magazine spread itself out on the floor, giving them a vivid close up of some young girl's face in mock ecstasy, naked body contorted on a picnic table, waist apparently made of tanned taffy.

"Henry," she said, pink jowls shaking. "You bloody pervert!"

Derek blinked.

"If I catch you with this degenerate smut again—"

"I don't want to live with a pervert, Mom. Throw him out now!"

"Emily, calm down."

"God, Janice, what do you expect? Just be glad he isn't building bombs in the basement or joining a cult. What, Derek? No funny comeback?"

"What did I say about calling me by my first name, Charlotte?"

"Get out. Just get out of my room. Now."

The door-chime jangled as the hag scuttled out. Derek walked around the magazine, locked the door, and flipped the open sign to closed. February slush had turned the outside world cold, wet, and grey. Cars cut through the filthy snow with a drizzling roar. Grit seemed to cover everything.

He finished the book, ran through the closing routine, then

picked up the porn mag and laid it beside the pulp novel. A warm smell, flowery, familiar, rose then vanished and he felt hungry. With lights out, he prepared to leave one last time.

"Derek?" Itches flared as he dropped the bag. He pinched his nose against the deep, sad smell, then turned.

Light flickered at the back of the store. A small teenaged girl stood between two giant piles of unsorted books that rose to her shoulders, fiction on the left, non-fiction on the right. Her grey shirt and blue dress were worn but not ragged.

Fear gnawed his spine. He coughed, still holding his nose, and picked up his bag. "We're closed."

"We know." A tinny voice echoed as if it had traveled from the far end of a long pipe. "And we know you're not coming back. That's why…everyone is helping me be seen."

Goosebumps burst on his skin. "Look, you can't stay. I have to set the alarm."

In her shadowy space, figments of her features and straight black hair flickered in and out of existence with the light. "I know, Jesse, be quiet!" Her face tightened. "There's no alarm, Derek. You use that line when customers won't leave."

His sucked his sore lip. "How did you—never mind. You have to go. I'm late."

"For what? The bus you never take? The long way home you always walk?"

Emily. She sounded as snooty as Emily did when they were kids. He crinkled the bag in his hand and walked to the phone behind the desk. She didn't move. "Either get out, or I'll call the police." He grabbed the receiver.

"I can't," she said, voice just a hint above a whisper. "I want to, but I can't. None of us can. Not alone."

Us? Lights flickered a little brighter then held steady. Pain engulfed her face. "Hey, are you ok? You need help?"

She nodded, opening her eyes. "We all do, Derek. We need your help."

He released the receiver. "Who are you?"

"Lucy Markson. We've never met. Not really." Her strained face eased and the light flickered again. "But you saved me, from the garbage heap and fire."

"What? I've never seen you before."

She nodded and the lights shook, then steadied. "I can't do

this for long. So please, help us."

"Help who? What are you talking about?"

"The books. The ones you…sensed. You know, when your nose gets all scrunchy. We're…we're tied to them." She bit her quivering lip and he released his. "We died with them."

Derek blinked and blinked as if to clear the questions storming his mind. She lifted her pale hand. "Let me finish. We all died, lost in these books. I don't know why, but we did. Marcus says it's because our hearts just stopped. That we died because we were…"

"Lonely."

The light steadied. An ounce of relief caressed Lucy's face. "I think so. We couldn't live on books alone. No one can. Not really. But we tried." Her eyes narrowed. "You don't believe me."

Derek inhaled long and hard and shook his head. "I don't know. I used to think…" He sucked his lip. "I used to think I could sense something. From books. But none of them had value. Not to the store. Except the last one."

"Henry says it was his favorite book," she said, looking into the dark stacks. "And she'd told him to pack them all up…and get rid of them. The smell was driving her nuts. He did…then he died, right, Henry?" She seemed to be talking to the books on her right. "Then she just shoved it in with a bunch of others. Packing him away."

Shivers danced on Derek's nerves. "Oh."

The lights dimmed and her eyes went black as tar. "Derek, please. The owner? He's not just letting you go. He's closing the store. We're headed for the fire." Her face wavered in and out the light. "It won't free us. But there's a way."

"How?" Even as he said it, he couldn't believe he was having his conversation. But he stayed still.

"You have to find us. Read us. Then we can…go."

"How do you know?"

Her face tensed. "Because Marcus vanished as soon as you finished that book." She pointed at the yellow cover of *Weird Heroes*. "I think it's because we connect with you. You're almost like us." He clamped his jaw. "But when you read the books with us, we're no longer really…"

The word came out dry and pasty between his teeth. "Alone."

She flickered. "This hurts. We've saved up all the strength

we've got. We need you to help us, get us out. Find us."

"How the hell can I do that?"

She tapped her nose as the lights dimmed. She faded.

He stood still, rubbing his nose against the itch. But it wouldn't go. He looked at the grey world of cold flurries. He'd breath free if he left. Sinuses clear. Empty. Gone.

Another bus passed by the window. His mind followed it home.

"You're wasting your life, Derek. All your potential. And you have no right to."

"Why do you always focus on him? I aced my finals last term, I'm volunteering at Mount Sinai, I'm doing everything right!"

"Not now, Emily."

"Oh dear, he looks like he's about to throw us the silent treatment. Not really a challenge when you have no friends outside that junk shop."

"Charlotte!"

He grinned, then roamed the stacks, breathing deep, until the books pinched his nose: *Alice in Wonderland, The Gulag Archipelago, The Princess Bride, The Bell Jar, Vincent Price's Monsters, Life and Loves of a She Devil, Dracula, Lord Jim, The Sound and the Fury, Lord of the Rings, The White Hotel, The Left Hand of Darkness…*

He ran through the stacks until the sweat swam through his shirt. His nose was calm. "Whew."

Then he glanced at the dark space of Porn City in the back. His nostrils flared. "Oh, fuck no." The voices rose as he clenched his eyes shut. "Shut up, shut the hell up!"

Arms full, he ran through and grabbed the one that made his nose itch. In the dim light he saw a *Playboy* from the 1980s with some Jessica Hahn wannabe pouting on the cover. Scolding voices fluttered in his mind before jangles filled the air. Books dropped from his arms as he shook.

Mr. Fletcher's nicotine stained voice peeled the skin off his soul. "Sullivan? Jesus Christ, what the fuck are you still doing here, running around in the dark?" He hit the lights and Derek shut his eyes. "What the hell are you doing with those?" His cigarette bounced on his thin lip.

Whispers rose from the books. He grabbed them, slowly. "I bought them. Last time to get the store discount."

Mr. Fletcher walked down the steps with a heavy gait, wiping the February wetness from his five o'clock shadow and pulling at his loose tie. "Better not be trophy hunting." He went behind the cash desk.

"I don't know how."

"Got that right. Just wanted to get the sales to the bank machine. You buy anything for the store today?" Fletcher bent behind the desk to the safe.

Derek crept to the door. "Just that Shadow book." He got to the cash desk, reaching for it. "Which I also bought."

Mr. Fletcher's rumpled head rose from behind the desk. "Not so fast, ass clown. Put that shit on the desk. Don't want you walking away with a few million in eBay sales."

What blood remained in his head turned white as Fletcher's sausage fingers ran through the books, searching, hunting for anything out of the ordinary.

Fletcher snorted. "This is garbage with ISBNs."

The itch was deep and shivering in Derek's nose. His hands flexed in spasms as he tried to hold still. "I want to…"

"What?"

His hands turned to fists. "Annoy my family. They hate this junk. Especially the fantasy stuff."

Fletcher held up the *Playboy* and the *Hustler*. "And the skin mags?"

He shrugged, breathing through his mouth. "What better way to piss off a house full of feminists?"

Fletcher's wheezy laugh pushed past his yellow teeth. "Shit, Sullivan, that's a good one. I could have sworn you were an ass bandit."

The itch eased as Derek inhaled deep. "Well, boss, now I've got proof to the contrary."

Mr. Fletcher shoved the cash in a large white plastic bag. "Well, so long, kid. Hope you find work somewhere soon."

Derek smiled. He left the store, chimes jangling behind him as the wind bit. The vroom of a distant bus pricked his ears so he ran and caught it. He sat down, wheezing, nose inflamed, and picked out a book at random.

'Alice was beginning to get very tired of sitting by her sister by the bank…' A tinny whisper thanked him as the pages crept on, the light of the bus flickering, the sweet smell of an unknown flower blooming inside him.

◊◊◊◊◊

The interrogation began at the kitchen table. Words filling his head like icy mist shot across a long, cold tunnel, but as loud as a bullhorn.

"Conrad? D. M. Thomas? Solzhenitsyn? God, Derek, are you feeling alright?"

"He's also got the perv mags! See? I told you he was a male chauvinist pig."

"Emily, that is enough. Your brother is not—"

"Fay Weldon? Who knew my little brother had such good taste?"

"But the perv mags!"

"I'll toss the *Hustler*," Derek said, voice dry, silencing them. "But I'm keeping the *Playboy*." He smiled at the empty seats at the table. "For the articles, of course."

Skin Like Shining Armour

by TOM CONOBOY

WHEN I WOKE UP I WAS IN SAND DUNES. SAND WAS in my mouth. Grass scratched at my eyes. The sun was white and burning. My body felt heavy, moulded into the sand like a body sunk into its coffin. I couldn't open my eyes and I concentrated on sound, but all I could hear was wind on the sea and water lapping on the shore and grass rustling beside my head. I focused on that grass through slitted eyes, on its browned stem where it was anchored in sand, at the roughness of its texture, sharpness of its edges. It shook—it seemed to me dismissively. My throat was raw, tongue dry and thick. The sun was too hot. I felt sure I would be sick.

When my eyes adjusted to the sunlight, and gravity loosened its grip enough to allow me to move, I got onto my hands and knees like a dog. I looked up and sniffed the air—the sea was that way, behind the largest dune. I crawled up it and lay flat, head above the horizon like a suicidal soldier, and looked at the sea, blue and creeping towards land as though seeking sanctuary. I could hear it and it sounded like a song, a windsong.

I had water but no food. At first, I hated the hunger because it reminded me of my body when I was trying to live in my head, but I grew to like the sensation of my body eating itself, molecule by molecule. I deserved that. The first night was hard, so cold, so long but never truly dark. There were too many stars wasting their light. I didn't think to make a fire. The second night I thought it, but didn't know how. The third night I had fire, but I didn't know where it came from. I sat and watched it till light.

After a while it is possible to read fire. First impressions are of individual flames, jagged, unconnected, but then, in the darkest of the dark, your thoughts begin to slide together and so does the fire and it becomes a single, flowing entity, a life drawn from death, born in destruction. You can read it, every action, but you don't know what it is saying, not about you, anyway, not about why you're here, alone, in sand dunes, waiting for an angel or for death or for some damned thing. That was when I was at my lowest. I thought then that I needed to eat.

When I woke up the next morning there was a fish beside the fire with me next to it. It was dead but it was looking at me, as though I'd done this. Its eye was black and it looked like it wanted to blink, like it was uncomfortable with all this. It had skin like a suit of armour, shining in the light. Its mouth was closed. Its tail was brown. I held it in my hands and it was cold, not quite slimy, as though if I held it in the water it could come back to life and its spine would twist and its tail would twist and it would turn and swim away and leave me behind, leave me with the cold, dark, pleading eye and skin like shining armour, roasting in the fire.

I didn't want to eat it, not at first. I had grown accustomed to hunger: more than that, it felt comfortable, as though I was cleansing my body. Such thoughts are like cancer. As the cold of night descended and darkness spread beyond the fire, I fought that cancer. I ate the fish. I wrapped it in grass and slid it onto the embers of the edge of the fire and watched their white and red force transform that fish. Its eye popped and bubbled. The silver of its skin tarnished brown to black. Its flesh turned to carbon, protein, flesh of my flesh. I ate. It was beautiful. Flames danced, I danced, I felt drunk with the power of living. I stared into the fire and saw life, saw myself, laughing, saw my world, growing, saw happiness. That night, delirious, for the first time I slept until dawn.

Every morning after that, when I awoke next to the remains of the fire, there was a fish beside me. Sometimes it was flat, sometimes round, sometimes silver, sometimes brown. I learned that wrapping them in different types of leaves changed the taste: those of the squat tree by the edge of the wood made the fish taste of aniseed, while the plentiful red-flowered shrubs with the bright, fat berries, tasted of honey and smoke. I learned not to cook them too long, that stuffing them with figs and berries and seaweed made them more succulent. My body filled out, I felt full of energy, took to swimming every morning in the coolness of the sea as a way of escaping the sun. I found I could stay afloat for an hour at a time, then two, then three. I explored the depths. I learned to hold my breath and kick and push downwards, into a mysterious, bubbling world of texture and silence where I felt welcome like a guest at a feast.

In the evenings I danced. I stripped naked and the touch of sand on my skin felt precious, the squeeze of it between my toes, its wind-whipped strafe across my calves, thighs. I planted my feet wide apart, bending low, arms spread for balance, and I felt a pulse of life run through me, one-fish-two-figs-three-leaves-four-flames, over, over, slower than a heartbeat, solid like a memory. It was deep and sultry, like a smooth voice romancing. It was everywhere, in my head, the sand, the sea, the trees. It echoed in the air, shaping and re-shaping itself in the wake of my dance, sliding around and against and inside me and holding me in its embrace like the kiss of a lover for the very first time. That's how I fell in love. This was how it was meant to be. I danced to the spark of the fire, to the setting of the sun, to the lingering taste of fish in my mouth, to the carefree knowledge of fish in the morning, and when it was dark, and when my legs were weary I lay down in the twilight and reminisced on the fullness of my day.

"Thank you, fish," I was accustomed to saying when I had eaten. "Thank you for giving me your flesh, for nourishing mine." It was a small gesture but it took nothing from me and gave me satisfaction. And then I would swim among the fish in the sea and they seemed to accept me.

The matter of who I was and how I came to be there bothered me little. In the early days I wondered. There was some vestigial memory in the shadows of my head which, if examined, might have become clearer, but I saw no need to probe. I had food and I had fire. I had swimming and dancing. This was life. When I danced, the ground and the air pulsed with something like music, but richer, more real, as though it was a part of me. It was the rapture of the dance, that was when I was living. And when I was resting, when I was eating, that was when I knew happiness.

I was aware from early on of the other. His fires glowed further down the beach and when the wind was from the east I could smell his cooking. His shouts filled the air at regular intervals through the day, harsh and staccato, and I could tell from this that he had not found how to ride the pulse as I could. I felt sorry for that, because it was a source of joy. He must have known I was there, too, but made no effort to contact me and we lived together, apart, for a long time. That was a good way to be.

When rains came, my fire would move under the cover of trees. Although it was cold, I found that the bark of the the tall tree with no branches could be stripped and woven into a pliable fabric. It became my coat, my trousers, my shoes, it brought me comfort. A fresh fish awaited me every morning. My dives went ever deeper and I came to love the variety of life which existed beneath the waters. Back on land, beneath a drying sun, the pulse of my dance rippled ever stronger through my body, as though pulling me into the fabric of the earth itself. I belonged.

"Thank you, fish," I said one day after eating a flounder with figs.

"Why do you thank the fish?" said a voice.

I turned. Behind me was a man and behind him footsteps, mazy, forming a giant half crescent all the way down the beach to where the other fire was.

"Because I've just eaten it," I replied. "It has fed me."

The man said nothing but watched me. He looked much as I must myself, I imagined, though I had only seen my watery reflection in all the time I had been there and was happy to forget what I looked like. He had a beard, long hair. His eyes were black and staring, as though they didn't approve.

"Did it choose to feed you?" he said. I replied I didn't know. "Did it give itself willingly?" I replied the same and the man turned away in disgust. I thought he was going to leave, but he stopped and came back. "Have you never asked," he said, "have you never asked how you come to have those fish?"

"No," I replied. As long as I had them, the thought had never seemed important.

"Do you thank the fire, the way you thank the fish?"

"Yes."

He called me a fool. He talked of many things I didn't

understand. He told me the fish and the fire were gifts and only a fool would thank the gift but ignore the giver. There was no giver, I replied. I saw no-one. The fish and the fire were mine.

They could not be mine, he said, because I had nothing. "You must understand that fish is a gift. What would you do if that gift was taken away?"

His face was strained, unhappy. He reminded me of the morning I first awoke on the beach. "You think too deeply," I said. I wanted to show him my dance. I felt sure he would enjoy it but, as I thought about it, I couldn't remember how it started. I tried to adopt my stance, wide-legged and low, waiting for the pulse, one-fish-two-figs-three-leaves-four-flames, but the man looked at me with contempt.

"My name is Mark," he said. He took my arm and I felt his hand like ice on my skin. It was as though I had been burned. I held it limply as he walked away, and I turned and looked at my fire, which seemed smaller in the dusk. I shivered, coldness infesting my whole body.

That night I sat by the fire as Mark's voice drifted loud and dull through the darkness. His fire seemed to glow fiercely in the night sky and I prodded more driftwood on to mine. I wanted to dance but I couldn't hear the pulse and the ground seemed flat, unresponsive. Flames flickered like a line of the dead and the fire crackled and groaned to accommodate the fresh driftwood. I longed to hear the sea foaming into land but it seemed out of reach, beyond the dunes. I felt a knot in my stomach, like a hunger, although I had eaten well, and my body was still cold. The memory of his ice touch still burned on my skin. As I lay down to sleep I patted the sand next to me, where the fish would be in the morning, or so I hoped.

lavender and chamomile

by LASHAWN WANAK

MY SON'S BIRTHDAY IS COMING UP SOON, AND I still don't have a present. Sure, I can go to the toy store, but I want something special to give to him. Very special. So tonight, I'm going to the grotto.

My wife helps me pack. Only when I get in the SUV does she speak to me. "Be careful." It's a longer drive than I thought. Two hours takes me to the edge of the forest. I kill the engine and grab the sack, entering it on foot.

Moonlight streams through bare, black branches, illuminating the ground in front of me. Still, I'm not a forest man. Twigs snap beneath my boots. Thickets rustle as I push through them. I sound like an elephant lurching through the undergrowth. Yet somehow I reach the grotto undetected.

It's one thing to hear the stories, another to actually see it. Grass, still soft and green, quiet beneath my feet. The lick of pond water at the grotto's entrance. The grotto itself, a rocky swell of ground no higher than my shoulders, the craggy mouth in its side, the darkness gaping within. Even the air is slightly warmer—winter's touch is barely tolerated here.

The makeshift sack feels buoyant—it's not much of a sack… more of a pillowcase, really. Already, the smell from it makes my eyelids droop, my head jerk with drowsiness. I don't have the coffee thermos with me—I left it back in the car, thinking it would weigh me down. So, holding the pillowcase close, but not too close, I hunker down by the nearest bush, forcing my eyes to stay open and on the grotto.

I don't have long to wait.

Echoes of playful squeaks come from within the darkness, followed by a few deep *whuffs*. Soon, small shapes spill into the open and amble to the pond gleaming a few steps away. I can see them clearly: a mother bear, no taller than my knee, and two cubs, brown fur glossy with moonshine. Too bad there's only two—with three or more, I could make the snatch easily.

Instead, I'm gonna have a fight on my hands.

Well, I knew that would happen anyway. Might as well get it over with.

I reach into the pillowcase, feeling for the chamomile. I don't want the other ones, yet too strong an odor, and it will spook the bears away.

Carefully, I bring the chamomile out to my lips. Even under my slight breath, their delicate heads dip, wafting their slight, springy fragrance.

Mother Bear's snout barely ripples the water as she drinks. The cubs tumble over each other, more intent on playing than slaking their thirst. Their horseplay carries them a little ways from the grotto's entrance, closer towards me. Trying not to inhale too deeply, I pucker my lips and breathe lightly across the feathery tops.

The two cubs growl, nipping each other's furry backs before backing off, panting playfully. Abruptly, one of them plops down on the grass and yawns, wide enough for me to see its small, pebbly teeth. The mother rears, water dripping from its snout, snarl rippling through the air.

Cover blown.

I charge from the bushes, digging frantically in the pillowcase for the lavender. Mother Bear gives three sharp hoots and the cubs scatter, the one that yawned weaving towards the trees, away from the safety of the grotto. I scramble after it, but for a stubby, disoriented little thing, it's fast. I'm bent double as I chase it, almost on all fours myself, breath coming out in harsh, ragged pants.

Pain lances my right shoulder. I stumble, plough face first into the grass. Mother Bear grunts, her breath loud and hot in my ear. Gasping, I yank her off. She's surprisingly light but extremely agitated, snarling and thrashing about, trying to gnaw at my fingers. I'm not too worried—they told me the teeth were too blunt to cause any damage. It's the claws I gotta watch out for.

More pain shoots through my left ankle. A cub has latched onto my leg, scrabbling its rear paws through my socks. Its claws are thinner than its mother's and far sharper I can feel them piercing the cotton, digging into the top layer of my skin.

This is the one I want.

I throw the mother as far from me as I can, then grab the scruff of the cub and pull hard. Like peeling off a furry, writhing scab—tears prick my eyes, but I get the thing off. As the cub writhes and squeals in outrage, I flail for the lavender scattered about me and shove it into the cub's face.

Instantly, its body slumps, its eyes glazing in drowsiness.

A soft moan makes me look up. Mother Bear had seen what happened, but instead of rushing forward in a second attack, she stares at me from the grotto's entrance, her remaining cub huddled next to her. She hoots again, gently this time, rocking from side to side.

Aloud, I say, "I'm sorry."

Then I pry open the cub's mouth and shove the lavender down its throat. Its cottony inwards twitch and pulse as I push as far as my hand could go. From the discarded pillowcase, I pull out the stuffing: more lavender, more chamomile, wrapped in cotton gauze. I stuff it into the cub's gullet, pack it tight with leaves, stems, flowers, roots. The cub convulses, its struggles growing weaker and weaker until I've nearly emptied the pillowcase. Then it jerks three times and stills, dark seeds and light fluff speckling its snout.

Gently, I close its mouth.

I lay it on top of the pillowcase and stand up, wincing at the pain and blood from my ankle. The remaining cub whimpers, but Mother Bear doesn't move. She watches quietly, without rage or remorse, just to see what I do now.

Most men would take off at this point. But not me. I told my wife—promised her, really—that I would do it right.

Taking a deep breath, I unzip my jacket. Unbutton my shirt. Pull off the undershirt. When I am bare to the waist, I kneel down and puff my chest slightly out so Mother Bear can see. She steps forward, cocks her head.

"Go on," I say, through teeth chattering not from cold.

I steel myself for her sudden pounce, the cold slap of pain

ripping through my flesh. I clench my jaw, squeeze my streaming eyes shut, determined to ride out the pain. When she leans down to bite, however, I can't keep the howls from tearing loose from my throat.

I was wrong not to worry about the teeth.

She chews, gnaws, rips, tears at my chest…until she stops. And though I'm in agony, I'm afraid to open my eyes, afraid to look down and see my beating heart exposed to chill air. I don't want to see it. I don't…I don't…

Hot moist breath smelling of honey and grass. In reflex, I open my eyes to see Mother Bear's face, her eyes squinted, measuring. The stories are right—they truly do mirror the universe, its ancient agelessness, time existing out of time. When certain she has my attention, she leans back a little to lift her paw.

Those claws…dark and slender, as long as my thumb, shiny with blood, blood. They are as dark and wet as her eyes, as hard and razor sharp. Mother Bear exhales, then, deliberately, wraps her other paw around one, working it back and forth until it breaks off. Hypnotized, I watch her lower the broken claw to the ragged, bloody ruin of my chest, to the flesh jerking and pulsing, exposed to the night air. Slowly, she pushes the claw in, like a thumbtack into a bulletin board.

To my surprise, I don't feel anything. *That's not so bad*, I think.

Then the world…the universe…*explodes.*

No one told me about this part. Yes, I knew what would happen, but they didn't tell me about the pain, the pain that turns everything white, that goes beyond shrieking, beyond howling, the pain that goes to the bottom of a mother's tear-rimmed eyes and dumps out into a vast galaxy sharper than moonlight, sharper than starlight, vaster than the vacuum of space, shrinking everything else to nonexistence, the grotto, the bear, my own beating heart, it all pales, all shrinks to nothingness except pain, pain, pain, pain, blinding, *screaming pain…*

I don't remember gaining consciousness. I simply register that the sky is purple, which means dawn isn't too far off. I'm on my back, the ground a soft, cushioning bed. Gingerly, I look down, but my chest is whole again, not a welt mars my skin. But the grass around me is wet with blood, and as I sit up, an ache flares in my heart like glass ground to dust beneath a heel.

Mother Bear is gone, along with her only cub. The cub I

captured rests on the pillowcase next to me, its features growing soft in the emerging sunlight. I pick it up and study its splayed limbs, its glassy eyes. Then carefully, I cradle it in my arms.

◊◊◊◊◊

The bear has its home on my son's bed. He's called it his 'bestest birthday present, ever.' He squeezes it and reads to it and whispers secrets in its ear. He carries it around by one foot, its head bouncing against the floorboards. At night, he snuggles up to it, never falls asleep without it.

Occasionally, he leaves it on the floor, its button eyes gazing blankly up at the ceiling. That's when I pick it up and carry it back to its usual spot. Each time I do, I hold it to my chest just a little longer, put it back more reluctantly. There are nights when I've taken the bear to my own bed, hours after my wife is asleep. I pull it close, feeling the fur tickle my chest, making sure its ear is nestled against my heart.

Someday, when my son won't care about this bear anymore, I'll take it back to the grotto. I'll take it back to its mother, who will be waiting for me there. Alone.

Maybe she'll let me keep the claw as a reminder.

Riding to Hounds

by Thomas Canfield

I WATCHED THE PROCESSION APPROACH WITH A suitably solemn expression. Henry was in the lead, wearing a purple mantle lined with white satin, an ermine stole and crimson sash, doublet and hose. In his hand he carried a riding crop. Two paces to the rear was his wife. Or, I should say, his current wife. Number five: the vivacious and charming Katheryn Howard, still dewy with the false promise of youth. Behind the Queen came an assortment of retainers, courtiers, hangers-on, sycophants, favor seekers, and various court functionaries. It was all quite colorful and exotic.

"Well, Master McIntyre," the King addressed me, "have you seen to everything needs seeing to?"

"Everything, Sire."

I opened the door to the helicopter. I still found it jarring, this juxtaposition of twenty-first century technology and sixteenth century quaintness. I could not reconcile the one with the other, could not resolve in my own mind how I had come to be there and why I was not dead.

I had been flying reconnaissance in Helmand Province, Afghanistan, in the dead of winter, hellish conditions by any measure, when the chopper got sucked into a downdraft. We went plunging towards the mountains, towards certain death, caught in a swirling vortex of snow that reduced visibility to near zero. I remember the thrum of the motor rising in pitch, desperately striving to regain stability. I remember the cries of my mates. Then there was a wall of vertical blackness dead in front of us and a thin sliver of light that offered our only hope of salvation. I made for the light.

Only I came out the other side, along with the helicopter. The others might have landed anywhere for all I knew. They might not have made it at all. I ended up in sixteenth century England.

Henry had some difficulty scrambling aboard the chopper. He was a heavyset man and not the most agile. I debated whether I should help him and decided against it. It was a delicate matter—you did not touch the person of the King without good reason. I still had not sorted out the nuances of when it was permissible to do so and when it was not. So I did nothing, always the safest course.

I climbed aboard. A courtier stepped forward, raised a trumpet to his lips and blew a rousing blast that echoed off across the greensward and down the distant valley. The pack of hounds was released, surging forward and baying madly. The hunt was on.

Henry gave me the thumbs up. I had demonstrated the signal for him on our first flight together a week ago. I reciprocated now, smiling, took the chopper up to around two hundred feet and headed south. The best hunting grounds lay in that direction. I watched warily as Henry hefted himself out of his seat, made his way round to the back. He bellied up to the machine gun mounted by the bay door, grabbed hold of it. I had shown the King how to operate the gun on our maiden flight. He had taken to the weapon at once. It was like watching a kid with a new toy. Old Blood and Thunder Hal.

The problem was he started opening up on anything that moved down below. He didn't seem to realize the destructive power the gun packed. We went over this one village, a drab collection of thatch-roofed peasant huts, and Henry let them have it good. Just poured it down on them. I don't want to come off sounding like a liberal or anything but I was pretty disgusted. I mean, they're his peasants and he can do whatever he wants to them. But wholesale slaughter? That was going too far. I finally got him to quit when I explained that I had limited quantities of ammunition. But I still got nervous whenever he got near the gun.

I kept the chopper down low, a hundred feet or thereabouts. I could do that back here in the sixteenth century. There were no powerlines or anything like that to worry about. The English countryside was beautiful: lush, green, unspoiled. I watched it slip by below us. We'd covered about thirty miles when Henry opened up with a short burst, laying waste to a cow grazing in the meadow below. It was a sign that he was growing impatient.

I shifted in my seat. I was never entirely comfortable when in the King's presence. Although I admired him as a leader I confess that his penchant for having people executed, the cold-blooded ferocity with which he could turn on a man and destroy him, chilled me. I was in his favour only because I had brought him the helicopter. It was an amusement, something novel. But I knew that, like past favorites, it could all change in a heartbeat. Henry used a man, manipulated him, and, when his utility was at an end, discarded him. My utility was about at an end.

The chopper needed to be serviced. It needed fuel and ammunition. I wasn't likely to find either in sixteenth century England. I couldn't count on another flight after this. When the chopper was grounded it would likely mean I would lose the King's favour.

So, I was face to face with the problem I'd been grappling with ever since I'd landed back here in the past. How could I best preserve the integrity of this timeframe and yet still avoid conflict? Henry was a keg of dynamite, wanting only a stray spark to set him off. He was also a major historical figure. If he were to be injured, or killed, might it not perhaps alter the course of history? But then, hadn't I already done that by showing up in the past in a helicopter? It was the old time travel paradox: cause and effect became so intertwined, so inextricably mixed one with the other, that it was impossible to distinguish which was which any longer. It was like a serpent swallowing its own tail. One could never find a beginning or an end or any point to logically fasten on.

Something caught my eye down below: an immense, dark shape. I banked the helicopter around for a second look. Sheltered beneath the canopy of the trees something was moving slowly. Traces of thick, grey hide were visible within the shadows.

"Yon great beast," the King called out. I nodded, gooseflesh forming along my spine. I would have to flush the creature out into the open. I brought the helicopter in low, skimming the tops of the trees. The noise shattered the woodland quiet, startled the beast. It broke into a clumsy, lumbering run. The hunt was on.

Henry pounded his thighs, enjoying the moment immensely. "Run thou spawn of Hell. We deem it just and proper tribute that all within our realm submit before our will, man and beast alike." The King could be endearing in moments like these. As long as his attention and, more particularly, his wrath were focused elsewhere and not upon oneself, his presence was a spectacle well worth beholding.

"Great sulphurous beast," the King lashed out against his quarry, "of hellfire and brimstone art thou made. And to Hell thou shall return."

I was grinning as I flew the helicopter, my own excitement at fever pitch. Flashes of horn and huge bony mantle were visible at intervals beneath the leaves. When at last the beast broke from the trees and into the open the King and I both exclaimed aloud in admiration and in awe: triceratops, last of the dinosaurs.

The immense grey form turned as we passed overhead. I stared down at the vicious twin horns that were thrust into the air. The incredible power of the beast was evident in its every line, its every movement. The creature had been designed for battle, for survival in a harsh and predatory environment. I let the helicopter hover above the meadow, unable to take my eyes off the sight.

Dinosaurs, of course, were no more native to sixteenth century England than were helicopters. I had been caught in a temporal anomaly and shuttled back in time. I assumed that the same was true of the triceratops, only it had vaulted forward. This particular timeframe seemed subject to quirks of this sort, rents in the space-time continuum. It went beyond what we call your basic inconvenience.

The King began gesturing at me to set the helicopter down. I frowned and, after seeking out a spot sufficiently distant from the dinosaur, complied. I knew what Henry was up to and didn't like it. The King's actions could be attributed to the insane English predilection for fair play. Any contest of might or valour or gaming had to offer one's opponent, in this case a dinosaur, a sporting chance. We could have taken the beast cleanly and without risk from the air. And for that very reason, of course, we didn't do it. Instead we were sitting in the meadow, the engine shut down, waiting for this great lumbering hulk of bone and sinew and mindless fury to descend upon us: fair play. The bloody English and their chivalry.

Henry began yelling taunts across the meadow at the beast, goading it. This seemed unnecessary to me. The triceratops was already coming in our direction. It approached with cold-blooded assurance, certain of its prey. A startled pheasant, darting out from under the beast's feet, failed to distract it. The triceratops' malevolent, unwavering stare remained fixed on the helicopter.

"Swine. Churl," the King reviled it. "Foul, pestilent scourge."

I cleared my throat. "Sire, the beast is well within range. You can drop it from here if you like."

Henry shot me a disdainful glance. "Master McIntyre, it were not well spoken for a Scot. What were the purpose if t'were so easy as that." I held my peace then, ready to prove myself as brave a cavalier as the King, if not so foolish.

"Spawn of Hell," Henry yelled at the triceratops. "Why do you yet tarry? Art meet to contest the field or not? Poltroon."

I think it was the 'poltroon' that must have done it. The triceratops gave a deep thundering cry and charged. The earth shook. Great tufts of dirt kicked out behind the beast. Its grey bulk bore down on us like fury incarnate. Henry clutched the gun, refusing to fire until the last instant. It occurred to me that we were both about to die. I could see the pitted texture of the beast's skin, feel the wrath radiating from its eyes.

That was when the gun opened up, a tremendous, continual clattering noise. The bullets sprayed into the dinosaur's face. There was a blur of motion, dust-shrouded chaos. Bullets ricocheted off the bony mantle, whined overhead. The triceratops was going down under the terrible firepower but its momentum carried it forward into the helicopter. The creature hit with stunning force. I saw a horn shear through the metal side, barely missing the King. The whole body of the helicopter lurched backwards, tipped on its side. The frame collapsed.

I lay there without moving. Waiting. After several minutes I crawled out from under the wreckage. I found Henry standing upon his slain quarry's upturned belly. There was a bloody gash down one of the King's cheeks but other than that he looked fit and whole.

"Well, Master McIntyre," he hailed me, "it were fine sport this. Truly, a sport to test the mettle of Kings."

I nodded wearily. I looked at the triceratops. The beast was history. It must have taken fifty or sixty rounds full in the face. What was left of it was not pretty to look at. The King would not be mounting this particular specimen over his fireplace. I did not even have to look at the helicopter. It too, I knew, was history.

"I'm afraid we have a bit of a walk in front of us, Sire," I commented.

"No matter, Master McIntyre. Horses will suffice where nothing better offers." Henry looked quite pleased. He was basking in his prowess with the machine gun, I think, delighting in the way it extended his reach and magnified his power. He loomed a larger figure than ever, having tasted the heady draught of twenty-first century technology.

Henry glanced at the helicopter. There was a speculative gleam in his eye, a gleam that I recognized only too well. He was assessing the situation, or reassessing it, measuring my current worth in a way that did not auger well for the future.

So, what does an ex-helicopter pilot do in a sixteenth century court? The choices, I discovered, were rather limited. I did however, by dint of my knowledge of flying, land the post as the King's falconer, tending to his hawks and to the hunt. It is a congenial duty. I harbour only one fear: some day, one fine Spring morning in May perhaps, a black shadow will appear out of the eastern skies beating immense wings in the direction of the King's court. The King will demand of his falconer that he tame this bird of royal bulk—this bird that will one day, in a future I have ceased to long for and ceased to regret, be known as pterodactyl.

MARY BETH'S PROPHECY

by CATHY C. HALL

MY SISTER, MARY BETH, HAS A GIFT. I WOULDN'T call it a gift, but Momma always says, "Now, Penny, the Good Lord doesn't make mistakes." Well, I can think of a few mistakes I'd like to ask the Good Lord about, but I didn't get all the way to the sixth grade at Andrew Jackson Middle School without learning a thing or two about sassing Momma. So I guess the fact that Mary Beth can see the future is a gift. Leastways, in Momma's eyes.

Momma believes that Mary Beth is a prophet, like those ones in the Bible. And if you know anything about those fellows then you know they never had a good word to say. That's pretty much Mary Beth to a T. If Mary Beth sees something, you can be sure it's gonna be bad news.

When Mary Beth got that funny look on her face, Momma dropped the frying pan and came running from the kitchen to find out who was the next goner in our little town of Pine Mountain, Tennessee.

"Mary Beth! What is it, baby? What do you see?" asked Momma.

"It's John Wesley McCutcheon," said Mary Beth. "He's gonna get a train injury."

"Lord, have mercy!" said Momma. She fell into the chair with a plop. Momma looked like she was about to throw up.

"Mary Beth," said Momma, "are you sure? Are you absolutely sure?"

"Yep," said Mary Beth. "Train injury." And that was that for poor John Wesley.

John Wesley's daddy didn't see it quite that way. It didn't take long for Mr. McCutcheon to hear the latest Mary Beth prophecy. And he was madder than h-e-double hockey sticks when he showed up at our door.

"Deborah," he said (even though everybody calls Momma "Debbie"), "that daughter of yours has gone too far this time."

Mary Beth stood in the hallway, taking it all in. Maybe it's because she has the gift, but you'd never know Mary Beth was just seven. When Mr. McCutcheon glared at her, she never even blinked.

"My son," said Mr. McCutcheon, "is just eight years old. He's at home right now, crying his little eyes out. And his momma is beside herself." Another glare shot across the room toward Mary Beth.

Momma looked about to cry herself.

"Maybe she's wrong," said Momma.

Now they were both looking at Mary Beth, who took the opportunity to add a little something.

"A train injury right before Halloween," said Mary Beth.

Mr. McCutcheon slammed his fist on the table. "Is that what you think this is, young lady, a Halloween prank?!" He jerked the door open and stomped out.

Momma and I looked at Mary Beth, standing there with her thumb in her mouth.

"You better be right about this one," said Momma. Which I thought was kinda funny. 'Cause if Mary Beth was right, little John Wesley would be trick-or-treating as a ghost this year.

It wasn't long before the whole town was talking about the train injury. The fact that Pine Mountain has no train station came up again and again. After all, as long as John Wesley didn't go anywhere, how could he die of a train injury?

But then, people started talking about trains and such, and the next thing you know, Mr. McCutcheon offered to give folks in Pine Mountain five bucks for any train they brought to McCutcheon's Furniture. Kids were hunting in attics, and sandboxes, and everywhere in between looking for trains. Some kids made twenty bucks off the deal. Mr. Leroy Tuttle even gave his Word of Honor that he would lock his antique train set in his storage house till November first.

But that wasn't enough. A week or so before Halloween, Momma walked in the door, busting with the latest gossip.

"Girls, you are not going to believe what Mr. McCutcheon has done now!" Momma set the bucket of chicken on the table. "You remember that Mr. Trane who lives on Third Street? Well, he's up and gone now! The whole family's moved clear across the state. Courtesy of Mr. John McCutcheon."

Mr. Trane's one of those guys who works on power lines. Or used to before he moved. So I figured this was pretty good thinking on old man McCutcheon's part. Maybe he believed my sister had the gift; maybe he didn't. But he sure as heck wasn't taking any chances.

By the time the Pumpkin Carnival rolled around, on the evening before Halloween, you could cut the tension with a knife. The last couple of days had been trying, to say the least. From the time little John Wesley got up in the morning till he went to bed at night, his mother shadowed him. That didn't keep John Wesley from being a brat, but so far, it had kept him safe from a train injury. Just one more day, and then everyone could relax.

As usual, John Wesley whined non-stop, even at the Carnival. I guess having your momma tag along all night long can suck the joy out of any occasion. But he was getting on my last nerve by the time we lined up to ride the Hay Wagon of Horror.

Mary Beth and I scooted up to the front of Mr. Cole's truck and found a bale to sit on. It wasn't a minute before every bale was taken, with John Wesley hopping up to the last seat at the end of the truck bed. His mother stood at the fence post with Mr. Cole's wife.

Mr. Cole drove the truck along the winding dirt road that cut through the field while all of us kids bounced along in the back. It was a stretch to call this ride the Hay Wagon of Horror when everybody knew it was high school boys dressed up in masks, popping up now and then as we passed by. But then out of the blue, Mr. Cole's dog, Bertie, took off across the field and high-tailed it straight towards the truck. Bertie must have smelled a rabbit or something, because she sure wasn't stopping for the Hay Wagon. If Mr. Cole hadn't turned his wheel when he did, we would've had one gen-u-ine horror right there in the middle of the field.

We all held on for dear life when the truck swerved. Except for John Wesley. He went sailing through the air, legs and arms flying every which way, till he landed with a thud. His pointy head smacked the ground with a loud wham! Poor little John Wesley didn't look so good. Well, that's that, I thought. But then his eyes blinked open and he commenced to moan. Next thing you know, goblins and ghouls and Mrs. Cole's wife and Mrs. McCutcheon, screaming her fool head off, came running from all over that field.

Mary Beth smiled a little around the thumb hanging from her mouth. Momma's little prophet was awfully proud of herself, watching folks crowding around the almost-dead John Wesley. But I wasn't the least impressed.

"Fer cryin' out loud, Mary Beth," I said, turning around, "when the Good Lord said *brain*, you thought He said *train*."

See what I mean about mistakes?

CRISP

by Erik Secker

NICK LAY ON HIS BACK. A CAPE COVERED HIS TORSO and a rubber vise constrained his neck. His head dangled inside the sink. A minor emergency had pulled Meredith away with the promise to return "momentarily." He studied the artfully exposed rafters above him. Bass thumped through the salon speakers. A nearby stylist and her customer discussed holistic food and Chinese medicine. He drummed his fingers against the armrest and tapped the footrest faster than the beat of the music.

Finally, the click of approaching heels.

A head appeared above Nick. But not Meredith's.

She had blond hair, the bangs of which covered her eyes. Three buttons clasped her white blouse together, the top button deep in the cleavage of non-existent breasts, the bottom an inch above her belly button.

"Hi," she said. "I'm Frankie."

She proffered a brown lunch bag.

"Would you like to pick from the 'Mystery Bag'? I'm promoting a book."

Nick shrugged a nod and waved an arm free of the cape. Reaching up, he read the block letters sharpied onto the bag.

CRISP

Notes From the Apocalypse: 10:00 AM to 10:45 AM CST

Nick paused. *The Apocalypse?* And what about the times? His was a 10:00 AM hair appointment. He frowned and looked at Frankie. Her bangs parted to reveal dancing green eyes. She wore a jaunty, crooked smile that leaned towards a mole on her left cheek. Cute. And then, because the pale skin blazed like a beacon and Nick couldn't help himself, he stole quick, darting glances between her cleavage and her belly button. He covered these attentions by reaching into the "Mystery Bag."

Out came a potato chip.

"A potato chip?" Nick asked.

"Don't you like potato chips?"

"Well, sure. I am a man, after all."

He winced. *I am a man?* Really? How cheesy was that? Would she think he was coming on to her? *Was* he coming on to her?

Nick shoved the potato chip into his mouth.

Umm. Thick, salty, and crispy. But also buttery. If he let it, it might actually melt in his mouth. Delicious. What was the brand?

He started to speak—either "good" or "what are these" or maybe a combination of the two—but realized that to open his mouth at this angle would expose Frankie to the slurry of half eaten chips no doubt still coating his tongue and teeth. He nodded instead and tried to project a smile both discerning and impressed.

She set the brown bag on the counter beside a jar of scissors and another of combs suspended in blue liquid. Then leaning over him, Frankie turned on the faucet. Her hip rested against his shoulder. She swiped her fingers through the water to test the temperature. When she judged it comfortable, she directed the faucet to run into Nick's hair. Then came the splayed fingers, drug past his temples into his hair and around the back of his head. And when her fingernails grazed his scalp and the soft skin behind his ears…

Umm. He closed his eyes.

Blat! Blat!

And opened them just as suddenly.

Frankie rubbed her hands together with squishy wetness. Of course, just the fart of a bottle ejecting shampoo into her hands.

"Um, so you're a writer?" he asked.

She started working the soap into his hair.

"What's that?" she said. The corner of her mouth crinkled towards the mole.

"Uh, the, uh, book you mentioned. You're a writer?"

"Oh. No, not really. Photographer."

“I see. So it’s a book of photos then?”

She nodded. He’d have liked to read her eyes, but the bangs shuttered them from view.

Her fingers kneaded as they lathered. They massaged his temples. They burrowed at the nape of his neck. Where they tugged his hair, the roots shivered in the scalp.

Umm. He closed his eyes again.

He continued to feel the pressure of her hip, shifting and rocking as she worked. Shifting and rocking, back and forth, as his hair grew a deep, thick foam.

“A photographer,” he said, somewhat remotely. “What kind of photography?”

Nick smelled her perfume. He’d never been good naming scents—except food, he was a man after all—but this struck him as having wild origins. A fragrance plucked from an epic landscape that rolled and swayed beyond what the eye could see.

“People mostly,” she said.

“Oh, like portraits?”

She turned the water back on and directed its flow onto Nick’s soapy halo. Her fingers parted and drug the hair, an echo of the previous wetting, but in reverse, undoing and scrubbing away what she had so recently applied.

“Sort of,” she said. “Though I work in candid shots. Moments that *reveal* something. That find a truth and show the subject as they are. Shots that are *real*, y’know? I’ve never been able to get that with a stool, backdrop, and the limited range of poses a person will bring into the studio: confident, sincere, likable, strong. I’m attracted to more *depth* than that.”

Nick contemplated the depth that he could bring to a photo shoot. Confident? Definitely. Strong? Yeah, sure. Maybe not in the muscle bound sense but definitely in the “can make tough decisions” form of the word. And likable? Yes, he would admit to that—he did smile a lot—but maybe that trait could be downplayed in his imagined photo shoot with Frankie. A number of “just friends” relationships in high school and college where he acted as confidant to his female friend’s relationship woes only to watch her leap back into the arms of her bastard boyfriend had taught him the sometimes perils of seeming too likable.

“You’d bring your ‘likable’ pose,” Frankie said, reading his mind. Nick opened his eyes. She'd adjusted the tilt of her head so that one eye glittered wryly through a part in the bangs.

He gave her a half smile. A smile he thought conveyed respectful disagreement with her opinion, but a smile that also showed understanding for how such an impression might have been reached, and definitely a smile meant for defusing any conflict that might arise when two people shared of difference of opinion such as this. Essentially, a smile that showed just how likable he really was.

She turned off the faucet and ran her fingers through his hair a final time, squeezing stray drops into the sink.

"Hot towel wrap?" she asked.

"Uh." He'd never been offered a towel wrap before. "Sure."

She produced a towel and stretched it over his eyes and forehead. It was warm, moist, and smelled a little of her perfume. Umm.

"Meredith should be back soon," Frankie said. "Help yourself to more crisps, if you'd like." Then she adjusted the towel to cover his ears as well. He felt more than heard the soft vibration of her heels drifting away.

And then, almost immediately, she returned.

The towel came away from his eyes and… Meredith stood over him.

"Sorry about that, Nick," she said. In a single, hurried motion, she righted his chair and swiveled him around to face the counter. Beyond the counter was a view of the street outside the salon. It was a gorgeous day with a deep blue crystal sky. The leaves had begun to change color, and soft greens, lemon yellows, and vivid reds painted the view. People strolled the sidewalks, carrying shopping bags, talking and laughing, walking arm in arm.

Then Nick noticed the brown paper bag on the counter in front of him. Umm. Chips. He smiled. As Maria gathered up her comb and scissors, Nick reached out from under his cape and extracted a potato chip from the bag.

Meredith seemed distracted. She kept changing her mind about the pair of scissors to use, replacing them into the jar only to pull them back out again.

"Strangest thing," she was saying. "That was John, my husband, who called. He said something weird is happening up north, where he works. But he kept breaking up and then the call died. And now I can only get his voicemail. He's never had reception problems in his building before."

She moved around behind him and started working. She tugged at his hair, rather hard, Nick thought. *Snip, snip, snip.* Pull. *Snip.* Pull. *Snip, snip, snip.*

But the potato chip was all buttery goodness. He let it melt in his mouth.

"Oh," she said. "Why did I grab this one? I *hate* this comb."

She reached around to replace it, and Nick took the opportunity to pluck another chip from the bag.

Crisp, he thought, reading the letters on the grease spotted paper.

He raised the chip to his mouth.

Boom!

A ball of fire exploded in the street beyond the window. And then another.

Boom. Boom. Boomboomboomboomboom. BOOM!

◊◊◊◊◊

Crisp: Notes from the Apocalypse, page 86-87 (photo): Man sits in a salon chair looking out a plate glass window. He wears a salon cape but has freed one hand to lift a potato chip to his mouth. Beside him, reflected on the street side of the window, a gold and black pluming ball of fire.

by Michael Bracken

I SCRAPED A DEAD KITTEN OFF THE ROAD YESTERDAY morning—a calico only a few days old. Over the years I've scraped all manner of dead things off the two-lane highway at the end of my drive—raccoons and rattlesnakes and most species of abandoned house pets—and I've buried them all behind the old stone barn.

After tending to the day's burial, I drove the DeSoto into town, stopping for breakfast at Irma's, where Irma herownself served me coffee thick as river mud, shared gossip about the preacher's daughter putting on weight like a milk cow, and talked about Billy Roberts getting him a football scholarship to Texas A&M.

Our town didn't have much, but we did have high school football. Seventeen straight trips to the state semi-finals had college coaches recruiting our boys. Them that were recruited played their four years, a few graduated, but, except for Wayne Earl Trout's two years in the Canadian Football League back in '90-'91, none ever went pro. Most of the boys came back home where the high school displayed their football trophies in a glass case just inside the front door and their social status was determined by whether or not their team took the state championship during their varsity season.

Football, though, remained the ticket out for a few of the boys. Doug Wilkins stayed in Bryan after college and has him a used car lot he advertises on late-night television. Milford Bates is selling insurance up in Dallas and Denny Delacroix probably did best of all. He got him a stunt man job out in Hollywood and we all watch for his name in the credits when we get to the movies over at the dollar theater.

"Full scholarship," Irma told me after laying down a plate of greasy eggs and greasier bacon. "My cousin is so proud of that damn boy of his, you'd think he's gonna bust a gut ever time he mentions the boy's name."

"Yeah?"

"Says his boy's gonna be the first one to go pro," she said. She refilled my coffee. "Real pro. NFL."

"He's got the arm," I agreed. I'd seen him play. "Could be the next Roger Staubach."

"Long as he keeps his head on straight," she said. "Don't do nothing stupid like Leroy Ledbetter."

Two years earlier, Leroy Ledbetter had been our first boy recruited by a major out-of-state college. Halfway through his first season, him and another boy got liquored up and skinned some tomcat they found behind the dorm and figured to be feral. Turned out the cat belonged to the Dean of the Business School and Leroy's back home now after spending six months in jail on a cruelty-to-animals charge.

I finished the bacon, sopped up the last of the eggs with a corner of my toast, and inquired about Irma's weekend plans, thinking we might catch the dollar show together if she's of a mind.

After breakfast, I hitched up my pants and strode on over to the hardware store where Ernie Ledbetter—Leroy's second cousin and second-team All-District Defensive Tackle during his senior year—helped me select a new shovel for scraping up the dead. Nobody ever talked about it, but I think everbody knew I'd do the right thing by whatever I found at the end of my drive.

We talked about the high school football team's chances the coming year.

"Defense looks sharp," I said. "Most of last year's starters are back."

"We gonna put any points on the board?" Ernie asked. "We ain't got no quarterback. A&M's got him."

"Yeah," I said. "Maybe it's time we all went back to church, started praying for the team."

"You seen the preacher's daughter?" he asked. "She's swoll up like a puffer fish."

I told him I hadn't seen the girl since end of the school year.

"Damn shame, too," he said. "Girl had a figure like an hourglass. Shame to see her losing it, start looking like all the other women round these parts."

"Girl's young enough to be your daughter," I said.

"I seen the way all the boys used to look at her. She didn't hardly walk down the street without ever boy in town panting after her." Ernie shook his head. "Damn shame the way she's let herself go."

We talked of other people we knew, then Ernie rang up my purchase and saw me to the door.

I walked down the street, carrying my new shovel and an earful of gossip, headed back to my DeSoto. I stopped when I heard shouting coming from behind Trout's Package Liquor.

"You can't do this to me," said a male voice. "Not now. Not after everything I've done."

A female voice responded. "Do it to you? You did it to me!"

I couldn't understand what the male voice said, but the female voice responded, "You think it'll be easy around here for me? It'll be…oh, God, it's happening again. I can't take the pain."

"You have to," the male voice said. "We ain't got a choice."

A truck engine fired up and I heard exhaust rumble through a pair of headers. Then tires squealed and a blood-red Dodge Dakota shot around the corner, a burly teenaged boy in a letterman jacket behind the wheel, a teenaged girl nearly glued to his arm.

I watched the truck disappear down the road, past Wilkins Television and Small Appliance Repair, and around the bend south of town. Then I threw the shovel in the back of DeSoto and drove home.

A few minutes past three a.m., I awoke to the sound of rumbling headers down near the end of my drive. I heard a truck door slam and then heard tires squealing. I listened to the truck's headers echo through the night until they finally faded away in the distance.

I scraped a dead baby off the road this morning—a Caucasian child only a few hours old—and carried it on the end of my new shovel around back of the old stone barn. As I dug a fresh hole next to the previous day's kitten, I wondered how long it would be until the preacher's daughter regained her figure and Billy Roberts threw his first touchdown pass for A&M.

For Sale

by David Melody

WILLIE STOOD BY THE TRACKS. HE LOOKED ONE WAY, then the other, seeing nothing but scarred walls of basalt. He took a final swig of vodka and tossed the bottle. The nearest house was at least five miles away.

He loved trains. He'd seen the Alps and most of Germany with a Eurorail pass, and on a side trip to France almost frozen to death in a cattle car. All that the summer after college when he was half-drunk on the freedom and whatever local beer he could find. Later, when he married and moved out west, it was always planes and Avis or taxis and tour buses, but no trains, no trains. Work, more work, and a wife who didn't travel.

It was almost time.

Willie, or William as he was known to his co-workers and to his neighbors at 721 Alder Lane, bent down to feel the track. Did it still work like that, he wondered, a quiet vibration? He didn't feel anything but it hardly mattered; the noon express was on its way. He almost laughed at the thought of a penny, and felt his pocket for change.

Earlier that morning he'd packed his suitcase, neat as always, with changes of socks and underwear for a typical five-day sales trip and left Meredith the usual note. Back in five, it read. Once, he tried xeroxing the note, so he could reuse it and save on paper, but thought better of it when she'd complained. He left it on the table under the cactus-shaped saltshaker they'd won at the fair. This time he'd added exclamation points. The suitcase was now in a dumpster behind the Waverly Building and his car at the airport parking lot. It already felt like a lifetime ago.

◊ ◊ ◊ ◊ ◊

Which trip had it been? Maybe all of them…

He'd been sitting by the pool. He never sat by the pool, didn't swim, and spent most of his time indoors at the bar where, underneath his brown suit, he was as white as alabaster and quite capable of cracking if mishandled; the alcohol barely helped. But after two hours of no air conditioning and no indication of when it would be fixed, that and the sense his calves were beginning to swell, he'd changed into his shorts and taken refuge outside under an umbrella, dangling his feet in the kiddie pool.

High above the hotel, scoops of puffy white cumulus floated, docked with others, and set off again, reminding him of his endless quest: piling up his sales numbers year after year. Eight months in and he was way, way behind.

"Duck?"

William shook the towel off his head, looked around at the other heads, marooned and motionless in the glassy-eyed heat, and resumed his position in the chaise-lounge. He'd been daydreaming about inventory, where everything shipped in one, fluid motion. As sales manager for Venture Electronics, his time was divided between parts and people. People and parts. Sometimes he wished he could reverse roles for a day: talk to the parts and stockpile the people—warehouse them and their problems.

The towel was no sooner back when a yank on his big toe brought him upright. A child stared back at him, an outstretched hand holding something yellow.

William tried to focus. His prescription sunglasses had broken the second day out and he wouldn't be getting another pair without company approval. His wife certainly wouldn't be buying him any.

"I'm sorry. Is Willie bothering you?"

At first William couldn't make out the face, backlit as it was by the sun. But the voice—soft, smooth and with a hint of confusion—pricked his attention. In the trade they called it Susel, short for "sure sell." When you heard a voice like that, you heard vulnerability, a guaranteed sale. He'd seen the studies, read the research, and applied the technique with mixed results during his car-dealing days. He was always analyzing voices. They could tell you so much. Sometimes too much, he thought, thinking of his wife. "Humph," William mumbled, climbing back from his sales figures, wondering where the curly-haired kid had popped up from.

"Come on, Willie," a woman said, moving away from the sun as she picked up the boy. The duck dropped from the child's hand, landed on William's shoulders and rolled down his chest, a wet stain in its wake. He handed it back to the woman. With his eyes shielded he got a better look.

"Oh, I'm sorry," she said, looking down at his shirt.

"Don't worry about it. I could use some cooling down."

"Couldn't we all," she replied. "Say, would you mind watching Willie for a sec? I'm going to the bar to get us something cold to drink." William watched the Cuervo banners flutter in the distance behind her. He could use another drink.

"No, I don't…"

"Think of is as a way to make up for your cleaning costs. Silk shirts and chlorine are not a happy mix."

"Well," he replied, not sure what else to say, as the child laughed and giggled and pressed the duck against William's nose, as if it was the funniest game in the world. The woman turned and headed toward the bar. She wore a sleek, one-piece black suit, with a red flower on the hip and deeply tanned skin everywhere else. What he remembered then, as now, was the scar on the back of her thigh, a thin white line, running from the inside of her knee to the swell of her ass. In his business, a defect meant disaster. But on her, it only accentuated the shapeliness of her legs. He wished he could feel the same way about his bald spot.

Ten minutes passed. He'd tired of baby talk and settled on squeezing the duck. Quack. Quack quack. Willie found this endlessly funny. William had forgotten about the time. Where was she? Jesus. He didn't even know her name.

"There you are," he heard her say from behind. He turned and saw she was holding three drinks pressed together against her chest, saw how the effort only accentuated her cleavage; the creamy rims of her untanned breasts brimmed just above the black edge of her top. He brought his eyes quickly up to hers.

"I can't…I can't do anything right today," she said. She put down the drinks and wiped back tears with a cocktail napkin.

She'd spilled the first set of drinks, she said, and now had to get back to her room to give Willie his insulin shot. "I'm sorry for all the trouble."

William sipped his drink and studied her sunglasses, so as not to be caught staring at her cheeks and neckline.

"This trip," she said, "it's so I, I could, or rather we could get on with our lives. I guess. Whatever that means. As if a trip could cure anything."

"Yeah," said William, hoping his trip would double his sales.

"Doctors think they know everything."

"I'm sorry," he said, now aware something bad must have happened, happy that whatever it was, it hadn't happened to him. Let her talk, he thought. That always helps.

"It's easy enough for Willie; he thinks heaven's just another adventure and that his Daddy's coming back. Like some cartoon character."

She continued and William listened with what he thought was an earnest look. He felt sorry for her, sorry she hadn't learned life was filled with trouble, and you lived and succeeded by having a backup plan. He stroked the boy's hair, its yellow strands felt like flax against his fingers.

"You and I have the same name," he said. He said his name aloud and looked up at the woman. "Maybe they've fixed the air conditioning. I've got to get back."

"And here I am blabbering on. Come on Willie, time for your nap."

"Willie go bye-bye," the child said, taking his mother's hand.

"You're William then, right? I'm Donna. Thanks for the looking after him." He watched her cross to the other side of the pool, sling a beach bag over her shoulder and pick up a pair of crutches. He grabbed his newspaper and towel and caught up with her.

"I didn't realize. Can I give you a hand?" he said.

"I try to walk as much as possible, but after a while the pain's too much."

William took her bag in one hand and Willie's hand in the other. He and Meredith had wanted kids, their own kids. They'd even thought about adopting but it never quite happened. Maybe it was his work, always on the road, and the fact that his year-end bonuses had disappeared. He and Meredith had wanted a lot of things

He glanced at his watch. Still plenty of time before his seven pm presentation; he might even work this Good Samaritan experience into his talk on teamwork.

Back inside the air conditioning was still off, and it was slow going with the crutches. By the time she opened the door to room 1215, William's shirt was soaked under both arms and sticking to his back. The heat made him dizzy; he made a mental note to start working out again. At least my room's on the same wing—a shower will feel good, he thought, as he placed the bag down on a table just inside her room. And that was the last thought he had for another twelve hours.

When William woke up the clock glowed a secret code: 5:30.

He'd missed his presentation. Or had he?

He did an inventory. He still had on his clothes, rumpled though they were, but what a headache. Plus his shoulder was sore, probably from sleeping the wrong way. When he moved, his arms and legs felt like sand bags. He'd had a couple of drinks poolside, to relax before the meeting. Three, four maybe, but that explained nothing. Was the heat too much at this altitude? Denver could be trouble in the summer. Where had he read that? Then he remembered the woman, walking back to her room, studying her back, the thin black straps of her bathing suit, wondering what it would feel like to slip them off her shoulders. And then a pain in his own shoulder.

Jesus. 5:30 A.M.! He splashed cold water on his face. What happened? Had he done anything? He'd been married nineteen years and in marriage, as in his job, the principal was consistency. (His few transgressions only proved the rule.) It wasn't the big sale, or the little sale, it was the consistent sale, a point he highlighted at all his presentations.

He tried to shake the grogginess as he showered, dressed, packed and figured an excuse for missing his meeting. Heatstroke? He'd have to read up on it in one of Meredith's medical books.

He called the front desk.

"Room 1215, the Johnsons?" the clerk said, "they checked yesterday." They? His hearing must be off. That wasn't heatstroke. Maybe booze. Maybe getting old. Whatever. He had a plane to catch.

Three weeks later, the first photographs arrived.

The envelope was marked "personal." *For Willie*, someone had written in big, black letters. He hadn't been called that since grade school, when he and the McKenzie brothers gave each other nicknames. Willie, Drilly, and Toboggan. He'd lost touch with the brothers but had heard that Toboggan, ironically, had been killed on the slopes while filming an extreme ski movie.

There was no note. Just photographs. He gagged. He stifled the reflex and gagged again. The photographs were of two people on a bed: a man and a child. Both naked. This isn't happening, it can't be happening, he thought, as he stared at himself and the boy named Willie.

◊ ◊ ◊ ◊ ◊

In the distance he could hear the train. It would be along soon. He bent down and placed a penny on the track.

DOING GOD'S WORK

by WAYNE SCHEER

ELI AND VERNON BROWBRIDGE ROLLED THE FAT MAN'S body from the trunk of their 1987 Pontiac Grand Prix into the hole in the ground they had just dug.

Eli spoke first. "I wonder if a dead fat guy smells worse'n a thin broad been roasting in a hot car trunk?" He grabbed a dirty handkerchief from his back pocket, blew his nose and wiped the sweat from his face. Dirt and snot streaked his cheek.

"You got me," Vernon replied. "Ain't never had no dead broad in my trunk before."

Eli put a dirty hand to his chin. "Sure makes you think. One day you think you're hot shit and the next day you smell like it."

Vernon nodded, but he paid little attention to his brother. He was enjoying the cool breeze drifting down from the North Georgia Mountains. As a child, he'd spend nights in his sleeping bag on the back porch falling asleep to the sound of chirping insects. Even with the skeeters, Vernon preferred nature to the room he shared with his brother, who would spend half the night asking him questions he had no idea how to answer.

"Vern," Eli asked. "How we gonna get The Fat Man into this little hole?"

Vernon circled the overstuffed grave. He tried bending Fat Man's legs, hoping the stiffening limbs might snap off. No luck.

"We gotta dig more. That's all there is to it. We gotta push The Fat Man on his side and dig this hole deeper."

It was hard work digging through roots and Georgia's hard clay. When they finally pushed the body towards the deeper side,

Eli wondered if that was enough.

"No," Vernon said, the body still stuck up on one side. "We gotta fit him in and cover him up good or we won't get paid."

Eli spit a mouthful of dirt. "Why's Georgia dirt get so hard in the sun?"

"Iron," Vernon said. "Georgia soil's gotta lotta iron in it. That's what makes it so hard." He always felt proud when he had an answer to one of Eli's stupid ass questions. "That's why it's so red. The iron rusts when it mixes with rain." He paused to let Eli appreciate his smarts. "I sure like the way these woods smell in the rain."

"Yeah. Me, too. Remember how when we was kids we'd run through the wet woods nekkid? Give Mama a fit."

They continued digging. It was noon and the sun took no pity on them. Their T-shirts stuck to their bodies; their jeans looked like they'd have to be scraped off.

An hour later they had dug The Fat Man's grave almost four feet deep. There was still a little hump along the middle of the hole, but the brothers decided it would do. They laid out The Fat Man's body until he looked almost comfortable and began shoveling dirt and leaves over him. A mound formed by The Fat Man's belly remained visible, but they covered the hole with more leaves until the mound evened out.

"You think we should say a prayer or something, Vern?"

Eli was back with his damned questions. "Wouldn't do no good," Vernon said after a few seconds. "Only prayer I know is 'Now-I-Lay-Me-Down-to-Sleep.' I reckon it's too late for that one."

"Vern," Eli had on his serious face, the one where his forehead wrinkled and his eyebrows met. "Are we bad people for doing this?"

Vernon answered immediately. "No, sir. The man deserves a grave, don't he? We're giving it to him. We didn't kill him. Now that'd be wrong. We just doing a honest day's work for a honest day's pay, just like Mama always says." He leaned on his shovel. "When we get the money, we'll give her some and she'll give part of it to Reverend Atwater. So the way I see it, we doing God's work."

Proud of himself, Vernon topped off the grave with more leaves and tree branches. "I reckon this here's as fine a grave as

The Fat Man deserves."

The two brothers stepped back to admire their work, threw their shovels into the back of their car and drove off to collect their pay.

◊◊◊◊◊

In less than two hours, a pack of dogs happened on the shallow grave and uncovered most of the body. Soon after that, a young couple driving down the deserted dirt road searching for wild blackberries saw the mangled corpse and called 911 on their cellphone. An hour later, Sheriff Erskine Calloway identified what was left of the body as Horace Latimer, aka The Fat Man, a local loan shark. He specialized in loans of twenty to one hundred dollars to illegals and gamblers, often demanding twice that if the loan wasn't repaid within twenty-four hours.

"At least we won't have a problem finding folks who wanted to kill him," the sheriff told his deputy. He sniffed at the body like a bitch in heat. "Sure is getting ripe out here in the sun. Don't reckon he's been dead too long, though. Can't see no gunshot or stab wounds, but it's hard to tell with all these dog bites. The man's so fat he just might have ate himself to death. But I doubt seriously he buried his damn self." Sheriff Calloway looked at his deputy who was writing furiously in his ever-present notebook. "You getting all this down, son?"

"Yes, sir."

"We won't know nothing for sure till Doc Robbins has himself a look-see. Probably won't know much then, if Doc already drank his lunch." He turned to his deputy. "It sure ain't like that CSI on television."

◊◊◊◊◊

Eli and Vernon collected their five-hundred dollars for a good day's work and visited their mother. LuAnne Browbridge had the sturdy, no nonsense look of a woman who raised two boys by herself after beating her drunkard of a husband nearly to death with a frying pan. Nothing surprised her, least of all Eli and Vernon. When they handed her one-hundred dollars in twenties, she asked no questions. She just reached under the top of her faded housedress and stashed the money safely into her bra.

"You boys gimme that kind of money, you got plenty more. Hand over another fifty."

The boys complied without a word.

She separated twenty dollars from the money. "This here's for Reverend Atwater. I'll ask him to pray for your sorry asses. Now y'all wash up good and you can stay for supper."

◊◊◊◊◊

The next day, Dr. Robbins said he couldn't determine cause of death for sure until the autopsy, but it seemed natural enough. The dog bites, at least, were post mortem. "From what I can tell it looks like his heart gave way," the doctor concluded.

"Well," Sheriff Calloway said to his deputy. "We got ourselves a di-lemma. If The Fat Man here died of natural causes, why'd someone go to the trouble of burying him in the woods?"

The deputy wrote the question in his notebook, adding three question marks.

Sheriff Calloway waited for an answer. When none was offered, he spoke. "My guess is someone didn't want us to know they was with him."

The deputy nodded.

"Off-hand, I don't know anyone who'd want it known they was with this sad excuse for a human being. So we got ourselves a whole mess of folks to question. Or we could look at it another way." He paused for the deputy to turn the page in his notebook.

"If you had a dirty job you wanted done, like burying a body, who'd you get to do it?"

The deputy looked up, his eyes flashing wide. "The Browbridge brothers."

"And who would do the job so half-assed the body'd be discovered before the devil had time to cart it off to hell?"

"Eli and Vern."

Sheriff Calloway smiled. "What say we have ourselves a little chat with the brothers Browbridge?"

◊◊◊◊◊

Mrs. Browbridge wasn't the least surprised when she saw the sheriff's car pull up in front of her house. "Eli! Vernon!" she shouted to her sons who were watching stunt bowling on ESPN.

"The po-lice is here. I don't know what y'all did this time, just keep me out of it."

Sheriff Calloway and his deputy removed their hats as they entered the surprisingly cozy Browbridge abode. "Ma'am," the sheriff nodded. "Your boys home?"

Eli and Vernon were trying to figure out how to record their show, but their mother's TiVO system might as well had been rocket science. They were pushing buttons and cursing when the sheriff walked in.

"What you boys up to?"

Vernon and Eli looked up from the remote. "Nothin'," Vernon said.

His brother added. "This danged recorder don't work."

"You boys trying to record this here bowling show?" the sheriff asked. When the brothers nodded, he took the remote and pressed the red record button.

"There. Now y'all do something for me. I got The Fat Man's body in the morgue. Found it out in the woods." He looked Eli and Vernon in the eye. "You boys know anything about it?"

"No, sir," said Vernon, speaking fast so Eli didn't say something dumb.

Eli still managed to get in a few words. "We don't know nothin' bout buryin' no body."

"Who said the body was buried?" He turned to his deputy. "You taking this down? We'll need this when we go before the judge."

"Judge?" Eli asked. "Why we need a judge?"

"Because murder and kidnapping and burying a body without a permit are crimes, that's why." The sheriff went silent, giving Eli and Vernon time to understand.

In less time than it would take a hungry fox to devour a chicken, the boys told him how Missy Taggert had hired them to put The Fat Man's body in the trunk of their car and bury him. "He was already dead," Eli explained. "We was just doing Miss Missy a favor."

"How much she pay you for this favor?"

"A hundred-and-fifty dollars," Vernon said. "We already give it to mama."

The deputy wrote furiously.

Sheriff Calloway took one look at the death stare LuAnne was shooting at her boys and figured they'd be punished enough. "Don't go spending that money or leaving town," he said, as he and the deputy walked out the door.

◊◊◊◊◊

Missy Taggert had been good-looking enough in her youth to have made a comfortable living as the town prostitute. When her looks went south along with her other assets, she married Darnell Grimes. Still, everyone in town knew her as Missy Taggert, especially the men. Darnell worked construction when he could get on with a road crew and tuned up cars when someone felt sorry for him or Missy. He wasn't home when the sheriff knocked on Missy's door. Since Sheriff Calloway had a personal relationship with Missy dating back to her former line of work, he had arranged for his deputy to meet him at the stationhouse.

Missy knew by the expression on the sheriff's face that this wasn't a friendly call, but she tried stalling. "Erskine, I haven't seen you since Tina Mae had her baby. How old is your granddaughter now?"

"She'll be two this coming winter, Missy. But I ain't here to talk family or old times." He wished he hadn't mentioned old times. "It seems we have ourselves a di-lemma. The Browbridge boys tell me you hired them for a certain job not long ago."

Getting Eli and Vernon to confess took more time than it took Missy to explain how she had been doing favors for The Fat Man to hold her over while Darnell found work. This time his heart couldn't take the excitement. She didn't want her husband to know, so she did what everyone in town did when they had a cesspool that needed unclogging or snakes under the porch that needed shooting. She called the Browbridge bothers and paid them with half of the money The Fat Man had in his wallet. She kept the rest.

"A hundred and fifty dollars?" Sheriff Calloway asked.

"Is that what they told you? The boys may be smarter than they look."

After coffee with a shot of rum, he agreed to keep the incident on the hush and hush if the final coroner's report confirmed it was a heart attack. After all, The Fat Man had no family and no friends who'd miss him.

◊◊◊◊◊

Sheriff Calloway had one more point of business to take care of before this whole mess could be wrapped up.

"Vern. Eli," he said, wrinkling his forehead to look as paternal as possible. Missy told me the truth and you boys are in the clear this time. There won't be no murder charges against you."

In unison, the boys blew air out of their puffed up cheeks. Eli wanted to shout "Yehaw!" but he thought better of it.

"But we still got ourselves a di-lemma." The sheriff rolled his tongue inside his mouth for a moment. "It seems Missy says she paid you five-hundred dollars and you say one-fifty. Since I believe her, that makes your statement to me—that my deputy had wrote down for the judge—what we call lying to a officer of the law. Now that can get you jail time."

Eli and Vernon just stared at the Sheriff. Even Eli couldn't think of anything to say.

"But we can work something out. Say you give me two hundred. You boys keep the rest and we won't talk no more about this."

The Browbridge brothers readily agreed. Vernon reached into his boot and took out a wad of wet, smelly twenties. He counted out two hundred and handed it to the sheriff.

Sheriff Calloway took the money. Before walking away, he said, "You boys stay out of trouble now, y'hear? I can't always be bailing you out."

As he slipped into his car, he smiled and put nine twenties in his wallet. The other one he placed in an envelope on which he scrawled, "Rev. Atwater."

Feeling the spirit, he mumbled, "Aw, what the hell," and added another twenty to the envelope. "Somebody got to do God's work."

Psychic Karma

by SHANNON SCHUREN

"WHY DO I LET YOU DRAG ME TO THESE THINGS?" LIZ grumbled, pushing through the throngs of people crowded into the convention center. "They're all the same."

"There's always a tarot reader." She pointed to a wrinkled woman in a turban doing a reading for an eager blonde. "She'll predict a birth or a death. The two things in life that are guaranteed. Freaking brilliant."

She eyed the stones lying on the counter of the next booth. "Runes?" she snorted. "Try rocks with scribbles. Only people with rocks for brains would take advice from them."

"Or," she continued, moving down the aisle, "we could get past life readings done. I may be just an average loser now, but I guarantee you in my past life I was Cleopatra or Elvis. Of course, that's only if the King is actually dead. These guys have proof of his reincarnation." She paused beside two women sporting sideburns and wooden beads. "A banana farmer in Costa Rica? Please."

She planted her feet and threw up her hands. "Donna, these people are all freaks. What the hell are we doing here?"

Donna blew a stray lock of hair out of her eyes and stared at her younger sister with a serene expression. "I want you to meet my shaman. She's taught me the power of forgiveness."

Liz looked away. "You go on without me. Forgiveness is overrated."

Jonas lounged outside his tent, underneath the large sign

proclaiming him "The Great Fortunato, Psychic Medium and Clairvoyant to the Stars." The stars included a local radio personality and a weather girl he'd slept with.

He eyed the crowd, trying to pick his next mark. He considered and quickly discarded a group of teenagers across the aisle. The girls would have idiotic questions about their prom dates, and the guys would give him crap so they could look cool in front of their friends. Plus, they wouldn't tip. Ditto the woman in the business suit with the crossed arms and hard stare. He knew a skeptic when he saw one. She'd have a bunch of questions designed to trip him up, and while he usually relished a challenge, today he was nursing a hangover. All he wanted was a nice, gullible sap willing to drop a wad of cash in exchange for a few meaningless promises about the future.

He spied a woman at the Elvis booth studying the crowd with a look of utter confusion. He'd seen her type before. She was here at the psychic fair searching for answers. Or meaning, or something. It didn't matter. Once inside, she'd become overwhelmed by the choices. He'd make it easy for her.

"Liz," he called, reading her nametag.

Her head snapped in his direction.

He hit her with the full power of his all-knowing oracle expression, staring deep into her eyes the way he practiced in the mirror every morning.

"Liz," he intoned, "I have a message for you."

Her eyes clouded. "Daddy?"

He almost laughed. This was too easy. He could do Daddy in his sleep. He furrowed his brow and cocked his head, as if listening to a far-off voice. "He wants you to know that he's sorry."

Liz swallowed hard. "He is?" she gasped.

Bingo. Always a winner. If nothing else, he was sorry for dying.

"Let's talk to Daddy," Jonas invited, sweeping aside the dark curtains and motioning her inside.

Donna scanned the crowd for a glimpse of Liz. She was beginning to regret her impulsive decision to bring her to the fair. Her own soul retrieval ceremony had been incredibly healing, releasing toxins built up in her body over the years of her abusive childhood. She'd wanted Liz to feel that same level of peace. But her independent, cynical, tough-as-nails little sister chose to cling to their poisoned past, rather than let someone get close enough to help her.

She paused outside the tent of The Great Fortunato. She'd seen the man outside only moments before. For some reason, the sight of his drawn curtains triggered a nauseating sense of foreboding.

She pushed her way inside to find Liz standing over the charlatan's body, a bloody crystal ball clutched in her hands.

"It's Daddy," her sister whispered when she caught sight of Donna. "The bastard just won't stay dead."

"Why do I keep dragging you along to these things?" Donna muttered as she knelt to help clean up the mess.

A Burning Question

by ANNA SYKORA

"HE WON'T TELL US WHAT HE KNOWS," SAID HELGA as the unmarked duty car rattled past stubbly fields. The dark road was deserted. When rain thudded the windshield, her young partner flicked on the wipers, which squeaked.

"Herr Ozal was upset, who lost his kiosk," said Selim. "He would have trusted me; you should have let me ask questions."

"I'm the senior officer," she said primly, smoothing her bleached blond hair.

"Don't I know, Kommissarin 'Battleship.'"

"Don't take that tone with me, Selim. Please slow down."

He did as they veered past a ruined barn: "Another candidate for arson."

"That reminds me, I want you to make a list of abandoned buildings and plot them on a map of Stammheim. You're good at computer chores."

He snorted. Helga stared out at the harvested fields. Here and there a bale of straw loomed up, encased in plastic to survive the German winter. The radio was quiet.

"Why don't you trust me?" Selim appealed. "That's the question; not who's setting these fires. We've been partners for six months."

"The longest of my life."

"Tell you what: you don't trust me 'cause my family's Kurdish."

"It's not your background, Selim. It's your impatience, your temper—" (he swerved to miss a leaping rabbit). "And the way you drive—like a maniac."

“That’s just what my mother says.” He chuckled. “I learned to drive in Istanbul, but I passed my German test.”

“Your inspector must have been drunk.”

He laughed out loud—a merry sound—revealing his fine, even teeth; and the corners of her stiff mouth twitched.

“Peace, partner,” he offered.

“I’m too tired to bicker. My roof’s leaking, and I spent hours on the phone fighting with the insurance.”

“If fire doesn’t get you, the water does.”

“Is that a Kurdish proverb?”

“No, I made it up.” Veering around a curve he picked up speed. Helga sighed and adjusted her seatbelt around her ample hips.

“Turks owned the kiosks that burned,” he mused. “Maybe, thugs from the National Party—”

“Nobody has mentioned neo-Nazis.”

“But you said Herr Ozal won’t tell us what he knows.”

“Maybe he’s afraid of organized crime.”

“The fact is, Germans hate immigrants.” Selim cast her a sly look; he’d say anything to get a rise out of her. “Even those who’ve lived here forty years.”

“Selim, you exaggerate everything,” she scolded. “Nobody I know hates foreigners. Without them this country would break down.”

“No more cheap gyros,” he teased. “No more juicy shishkebobs.” Their wrappings littered the car.

The radio crackled: “Car 22, assist at a fire in Heinrich Heine Street—at Peking Gardens. A family lives upstairs. ” Selim whooped and pulled an illegal U-turn. Scowling, Helga tightened her seatbelt.

“I love this job,” he sang, swerving around a curve.

◊◊◊◊◊

Flames rippled from the old brick-and-beam farmhouse holding “Peking Gardens.” A woman in a bathrobe stood in the street, clutching a bundle and screaming in Chinese. Red-overalled firemen hosed the flames. Valves flickered on their gleaming pumper-truck, its steel shutters rolled up high.

“What’s the matter?” Helga grabbed the woman’s arm—her bundle a baby—and steered her to the far curb, near where Selim was directing traffic.

"My husband, my little daughter—inside." Through the smoke they glimpsed a man balancing a child in pink pajamas on an upstairs sill. Flames roared behind them.

"Mommy!" The girl reached out to her, as firemen spread a net.

"Can't wait for the ladder-truck—toss her down!" their burly captain shouted. Her father held her dangling, let her fall. She shrieked as she bounced on the net—and Selim groaned, his handsome face twisting.

"What's the matter, man?" Helga demanded.

"I had to jump like that, once."

"Well, pull yourself together." She turned to the shivering woman: "Don't be afraid; more help's on the way." But her husband had disappeared. As the roof collapsed, he leaped out a different window, landing in a hedge on his back.

"Lee, Lee," the woman sobbed, and her baby started to wail. Firemen slid a stretcher under the man, who raised one scorched hand and let it fall. He wore blue jeans and one slipper. His wife ran to him, almost dropping the baby.

"Hateful people do this," spat Selim.

"Wait, it could be insurance fraud," said Helga. "I live around the corner, and this Peking Garden never bloomed. The food's lousy, and they let litter pile up outside in the beer garden."

"This was no accident. It's burning too fast."

"Let's see what our experts say."

◊◊◊◊◊

Herr Dackel was short, with a bristly grey moustache and oval glasses. His pointed shoes shone like mirrors.

"Thanks for assisting us." Helga leaned forward at her desk in the old brick station house, where computer screens peeked from partitioned cubicles. In a corner two uniformed officers were arguing about a soccer game.

"My pleasure, Kommissarin Schneider," replied the insurance adjustor. "I'm always pleased to help our police."

"Your conclusions?"

"Suspicion of arson, in all three incidents."

Perched on a chair, Selim blew out his breath.

"First, the most recent, at Peking Gardens. The polyurethane foam in booths and chairs provided ample fuel. The blaze started in or near a wall downstairs, so I thought first of an electrical fire. I also considered whether a smouldering butt could have started it, hours after closing. But our lab found distinct traces of gas in the dining room floor."

"There was no sign of a break-in," Helga observed.

"More reason to suspect an inside job."

"Why would the owner endanger his family?" Selim broke in, getting up. "He has a baby and a little girl, too."

"Maybe he didn't mean to," said Herr Dackel. "Gas is a treacherous accelerant; it can lead to explosions, or to fires rapidly sweeping out of control. Pros rarely use it."

"The owner's wife told us her husband was depressed," said Helga. "Last month he took out two policies: one on the restaurant, the other on his life."

"What about our Turk-owned kiosks?" Selim asked impatiently.

"A similar modus," said Herr Dackel dryly, crossing his stubby legs. "Our lab found traces of gas inside the bundles of scorched newspapers. A pro knows to moisten just the outside, so no traces remain."

"I can't believe people would risk their families—even for pots of insurance money."

"What about organized crime?" asked Helga. "Maybe these jobs aren't masterpieces, but can't they be the work of a single band of thugs?"

"Extortionists?" Herr Dackel studied the stains in the old-fashioned plaster ceiling. "Some have been known to prey on foreigners. Last year, there was a case in Hamburg..."

"Neo-Nazis prey on immigrants," Selim interrupted. "Who want to drive non-Germans out of town, and label Stammheim 'Foreigner-Free.'" Herr Dackel squinted up at the swarthy officer pacing the cubicle like a caged tiger. "I wouldn't know about that. We've never had such a case."

◊◊◊◊◊

After tanking up his battered, blue Honda, Selim strode towards the station's store. On second thought, he turned back and stuffed his service revolver into the glove compartment.

After paying the pretty cashier, he asked, "By the way, is Rolf Messer around?"

“Whaddya want with him?” she sneered.

“To talk about a matter of common interest.”

“What can we have in common?” a deep voice boomed, and the cashier tittered. A muscle-bound skinhead stepped in from a storeroom, carrying a metal rack.

“It’s no secret you head the National Party’s local chapter.”

“Anyone can read that in the internet,” Rolf retorted, whose initials were tattooed on the back of his hands in Gothic letters.

“Know anything about the fires in immigrant-owned businesses.”

“If I did, I sure wouldn’t tell you.” Rolf filled maps into his revolving tower, crowned with the sign: “Be prepared: Buy Meyer Maps.”

“If I were a cop, would you respect me?” hissed Selim.

“Shit foreigner.”

Selim punched him in the mouth, and the cashier screamed. Rebounding, Rolf bashed him over the head with the tower, and maps flew around like playing cards. Selim crumpled sideways against a shelf of snacks, which collapsed; he landed on the floor.

Rolf wiped his mouth with his hand, and stared at the blood: “Better call the police; he started it. You saw.”

◊◊◊◊◊

“Selim, I’ll do what I can for your hearing,” Helga told him glumly on the phone. Her colleagues had gathered around her cubicle, and grizzled Detective Schmidt was grinning with Schadenfreude. “Plainly you were at fault.”

“I shouldn’t have hit him,” her partner mourned.

“Better still, you never should have questioned him without consulting me. There’s no evidence linking the National Party—”

“But you always say I need to develop my own sources for information—”

“Selim, only you would try to question a rancid Nazi, who isn’t even a suspect. Your stupid brawl made the *Picture News*. Our chief is furious, and embarrassed.”

“I’m sorry, Helga.”

“Too late, you’re sorry,” she scolded.

Iwo Schmidt made a throat-slitting gesture and winked.

“I want you to know something,” said Selim sadly.

“Make it snappy. I’ve got a ton of work.”

“Not that it excuses what I did…When I was a child, in Kurdistan, the Turkish army burned our village. I had to jump out a window, just like that girl. Helga, I started flashing back…”

“So you’re claiming you’re a victim, man? You’re not responsible for picking that fight?”

“Never mind,” he groaned. “I should’ve known I’d get no sympathy from my partner.”

“Selim, like I said, I’ll do what I can,” she said in a gentler tone. “They’re probably going to suspend you though. And make you take anger management training.”

Cursing in Kurdish, he hung up, and Helga shook her head. Iwo—who’d never liked her noisy partner—flashed her a thumbs-down.

“Oh, come on, guys,” she appealed to her colleagues, all of them men. “Don’t wish the youngster in a bigger pot of grease.”

“They should shove him back where he comes from,” said Iwo.

Glaring, she almost called him an old donkey; but her phone burbled and she picked it up.

“Kommissarin Schneider,” growled the clerk downstairs who sorted members of the public like parcels, “Mehmet Ozal wants to see you, whose kiosk burned. He doesn’t have an appointment, he says.”

“Send him up.”

“He seems upset.”

“So’s everybody.” She smoothed her freshly bleached hair, which fell like a curtain to her shoulders exactly. (Longer’s not allowed).

Soon her frail visitor stepped from the elevator, his shoulders bowed and his eyes darting nervously. She shook his gnarled hand in her big, fleshy one and felt his hesitation. When she led him to her cubicle, he stared at the clutter of files on her desk.

“Mr. Ozal, may I take your overcoat?” He shook his head ‘no,’ and her heart sank. “Well, please sit down.” She pointed at the plain metal chair next to her desk. “What brings you to me?”

The wizened old man sat down, but did not lean back. “Kommissarin, I read about your partner in the *Picture News*.”

“Bad news travels fast.”

“I just wanted you to know that he’s an upstanding and good-hearted young man. Such a comfort to my family after the fire."

"Would you dictate a testimonial?" she queried. "His disciplinary hearing's coming up on Friday."

"Of course, of course…There's something else. Are we private here?"

"Not exactly. Shall we go to the conference room?"

"Never mind." He hesitated, wringing his hands. She rolled her chair closer; he flinched away. Drumming with her feet, she tried to smile, and he suddenly bent his head and muttered: "Selim thinks that the National Party's behind our fires. He's wrong."

"And how do you know?" she asked with interest.

"The men who…threatened me were Russians. My second cousin owned the other kiosk, and they broke his finger."

"Are we talking about extortion?"

"I can't tell you more," he whispered. "I worry about my sons and their children. We're a big family, with many targets. You check out the Russians in Leinau Street. Ask about Ivan the Chopper. " He stood up.

"Wait, Herr Ozal. What about your testimonial?"

The old man retreated, casting anxious glances, and scuttled down the stairs.

◊◊◊◊◊

She parked the duty car across from the rain-stained warehouse in Leinau Street, which sported a crudely-lettered sign, "Pavlova's Second Hand Paradise." There was some neater Cyrillic writing underneath. Many Russians in Stammheim speak little German.

"What a dump," grumbled Detective Schmidt, unfolding his long, bony legs from the passenger side.

The main door stood agape, despite the cold, and they stepped into a long and low-ceilinged room lit by bulbs in sockets and crowded with old wardrobes. Just like Grandma's, Helga thought. Who'd want them now? Foreign families counting their pennies? Paradise: your choice of fifty, missing their knobs.

"Can I help you," asked a middle-aged man with a heavy Russian accent. One eye drooped, and the knees of his pants were shiny.

Iwo flashed his police ID. "We'd like to speak with your proprietor."

“Got a warrant?”

“We don’t need one for a friendly conversation,” Helga pointed out.

The Russian hesitated, scowling. “Frau Pavlova’s in her office. This way.” They trailed him through a warren of musty rooms crammed with third-hand furniture. Ghostly congregations of ill-matched chairs waited wistfully. Cracked mirrors in ornate frames hung crooked, or lay stacked in heaps. Who’d want all this junk? thought Helga. Maybe people burn it in their stoves.

Rain rattled on the roof as they followed the droop-eyed man up rickety stairs. On the top floor, behind a partition of sawed-off doors, an elderly woman sat clicking away at an abacus. When he said something in Russian she turned her papers over, and peered up at her visitors through thick, rectangular glasses.

“Frau Pavlova?” Helga asked politely.

“Nadia Pavlova, that’s me.” She stood up, a trim figure barely reaching Helga’s shoulder. “Welcome to my paradise, officers. Of anything you want, we’ve got one hundred.” She wore a high-buttoned blouse and an apricot cardigan. Fashionable earrings glinted on her ears.

“Detectives Schmidt and Schneider, of Stammheim-North,” Helga said pleasantly. “We’d like to ask you a few, friendly questions.” Nadia nodded to her assistant, who plodded back down the stairs.

“Please sit down,” she urged, fussily arranging three straight-backed chairs from her stock. She chose the one with the ungashed seat, and the detectives sat down facing her.

“We’ve received an anonymous tip,” Helga began, “linking some recent fires with a Russian gang.”

“I don’t know anything about that,” said Nadia flatly. The pupils of her heavy-lidded eyes contracted.

“Ever heard of Ivan the Chopper?” Iwo got to the point.

“Sounds like a Russian fairy tale.”

“We’ve reason to believe a gang headed by this Ivan is extorting money from immigrants,” he said, and Helga studied the old woman’s face. Nobody you’d pick out of a crowd—or a line-up. Still, the coldness of her gaze, the stony set of her jaw suggested a harsh will. And big criminals come in the smallest packages.

“What has any of this to do with me, or my business?” asked Nadia airily. “I never heard of such a person.”

"Are you quite sure?" Iwo demanded.

"Do give me your card, officer," she replied coquettishly. "I'll be sure to call you if I hear anything." Helga flinched as he handed Nadia his card and wished her a pleasant evening.

She felt the old woman's steely eyes in her back as she retreated with Iwo. Out of earshot, Helga complained: "I would have liked to ask more questions."

"It's late, and I'm dying for a gyro."

A sleek black Mercedes had parked behind their unmarked car. With a nod to them, the droop-eyed man got in and drove away.

"Maybe it's second hand, too," said Helga.

◊◊◊◊◊

Late that evening she paid a visit to Otto's Cosy Bar. She found Hans Warner, her favorite informant, alone at the back of the smoke-laden room. He smiled at her almost shyly, then stood up and pumped her hand. His pale blue eyes looked bloodshot, and his breath smelled like an ashtray rinsed with schnaps.

Sitting down, she told the bored-looking waiter, "I'd like an alcohol-free beer."

"Always so careful," Hans rasped in his chain-smoked voice.

"I still have to drive home. Got anything for me on a Russian gang in Leinau Street?"

"That depends." He tossed off his schnaps and set the shot glass down.

"I've got fifty euros that I don't need."

"Always such a tight-wad. Even as a kid you'd hoard all your pennies in a piggy bank."

She rolled her eyes. "Out with it, Hans. You do know something." She slid a folded banknote under his coaster, which he palmed off the table with a practiced swipe.

"There's a gang alright, and that junk store's their front. The Russians are so bloody, our skinheads fear them. Helga, this country's going to the dogs."

She smiled patiently and drummed her feet. "What lines of business are our Russians in?"

"Gun-running from the Wild East…And strong-arming foreign businesses, I guess. Maybe some drug sales, too. They've always got a couple of trucks driving around, picking up furniture."

"They've got a Mercedes with custom leather."

"Russkies are crazy about fast cars. Hear about the sailors who drove off the pier in Hamburg? They both drowned."

"I read about that in the Picture News... Have you heard anything about an 'Ivan the Chopper?'" Frowning, he held his empty glass up to the light. "I may have another twenty Euros here."

When the waiter brought her beer, Hans ordered another schnaps. It came at once, and he tossed it off.

"Well?" she prodded. "You know it's not polite to keep a lady waiting."

"The Chopper rules his gang with a cleaver. Chops fingers off when the guys disobey."

She took a sip of beer and shook her head. "Sounds like one of your underworld legends."

"No, it's true. Helga, we never should have let those gangsters come into the country. They're spoiling everything." His voice rose, and she peered around the room. Quite drunk, he might be making up stories. Two black men in suits at the bar studied him; she waited till they turned back to their drinks before slipping him another banknote.

"Germany's going to the dogs," Hans lamented, sliding it into his breast pocket.

◊◊◊◊◊

Dark smoke rose like a mushroom cloud from the hovel in the woods. Three ragged squatters wandered away, muttering in Polish. Several locals stood watching the team of firemen hose the blackened walls. Their fire truck had backed down a bicycle path and barely fit between two mossy oaks.

"Nobody'll miss those bums," announced an elderly lady in a red fox hat.

"I'm glad they burned their old place down," retorted a plump teen with silver studs in her nose.

Iwo Schmidt stood next to Helga. Both wore trench coats, their collars turned up high. "We can assume right-wingers are behind this." His breath puffed out in clouds. "Anyone who tosses a Molotov cocktail in broad daylight wants publicity."

"I don't believe it," she said calmly. "Our skins have other things in their empty skulls. Tomorrow's the big soccer game with Italy."

"Then what's the point of this fire?" he asked condescendingly, as they strolled back to the duty car.

"Maybe it's an effort to draw us off the scent."

"You've got a wild imagination. I learned long ago to keep things simple." She smoothed her wind-mussed hair. "Some things are simple, after all," he leered, folding himself into the driver's seat. "Cat and mouse. Man and woman."

She turned her head and stared out at the golden sunset between the trees. Twice divorced, this rack of bones had been chasing her ever since her own marriage died…He never trimmed his nose hairs. Like her ex.

◊◊◊◊◊

Later, speeding through the night alone, she made an illegal call on her cell phone:

"Selim, I'm sorry," she told his voice-mail. "You were right about bias in the precinct. I'm on my way to a tipster, with more on the Russians. Talk to you soon."

Rain fell in torrents as she swung into a deserted street behind Stammheim's freight railroad station. Why had she called him? She felt a wave of lonely yearning, and blinked her eyes. She didn't trust him? She didn't trust herself. She needed to control everything. This had wrecked her marriage.

She parked in a closed Thai restaurant's lot, next to the cavernous underpass. Hans would wait on the walkway, on the downtown side. A train rumbled overhead as she splashed through puddles, and her heart skipped a beat. She'd left her revolver in the car, but she trusted Uncle Hans.

Halfway through the underpass a man was kneeling on a piece of cardboard. Now why would Hans play a homeless man? He loved warmth and comfort.

"Hey, Uncle," she cried, and her voice echoed weirdly. "There must be a warm bar open somewhere." She stepped closer. "What, are you drunk?" She patted his head and he lolled back—the fingers of one hand just stumps.

As she lurched backwards, strong arms grabbed her, and a foul-smelling wad slapped over her face. Chloroform…Her legs sagged under her, even as her mind blazed. Tricked.

◊◊◊◊◊

Rotten straw smell…Cold air gusted, and tiny frozen kisses stung her face. Her wrist ached, fastened overhead; and something clanked. She opened her eyes to darkness, and drew a deep breath that chilled her lungs. Thin light was seeping down; slowly, her eyes adjusted.

She lay on a pile of sodden straw next to a crumbling wall. A few snowflakes drifted down like dust from the gap in the ruined barn's roof. She was handcuffed to the bracket of a manger, her ankles securely strapped with duct tape.

Stains on the straw…A severed thumb poked out. She shuddered; they'd tortured poor Hans. And nobody in Stammheim knew where she was. Nobody but them.

A car door slammed; Russian voices were quarrelling. Shutting her eyes, she willed herself limp and waited, breathing slow.

A light dazzled her as a hard foot nudged her side. Framed by the doorless stall, Nadia Pavlova grinned down, pointing a flashlight. The old woman wore a stylish, long wool coat, trimmed with sleek black fur.

"You're Ivan, aren't you?" Helga exclaimed, and Nadia laughed derisively.

"Don't ask me more questions, Kommissarin. I'll tell you something: your Hans wanted money, to tell what he told you. That's all you Germans care about—money."

"Don't you understand, if you kill me too, the police will come swooping down. You'll rot in prison, Nadia; you'll die there." Helga clanked her cuff against the bracket.

"Who are you to tell my future?" Nadia shone the light in her eyes. "I survived Communism in Kazakhstan. I survived immigration with my four stupid sons."

"This is a country with rules and laws. You'll pay for your crimes, I promise you."

"There's only one law on earth: survival. And you're going to die, Kommissarin—roasted like a piggy in a pit." Over her shoulder Nadia spoke sharply in Russian.

Into the barn stepped the droop-eyed man, carrying a black canister. He was missing a pinky. Quickly he shook gasoline along the walls, almost stumbling over a rusty axe.

Nadia lit a cigarette, took one puff and blew the smoke in

Helga's face. Then she tossed the cigarette into a puddle, clapped her son on the back, and hurried away.

"We have laws in this country!" Helga shouted, tugging at the sturdy bracket. By the time the wall around it burned…

She started to cough from the heaving smoke. Overhead she heard a scrabbling. Selim hung from the gap, dropped to the straw:

"Aren't you glad to see me?"

"Help me—we need to break this. Over there, that axe!" Helga pointed. When he grabbed it the rotten handle fell off. Cursing in Kurdish, he gripped the head with both hands and smashed it on the manger; then grimaced.

"Wrap your hands in your jacket," she pleaded, as the flames blazed hot and high. Sweat pearled on his face, and with a heavy thud he struck again. Something pinged off the axe head. "Hurry!"

He struck a third time, and the manger broke away. She yanked her arm free and hopped two steps, hobbled by the tape. Grabbing her he hefted her over his back and staggered towards the open door, as more bullets pinged overhead.

Safe outside they heard shouting in Russian, and a motor roared.

"We'll tail them!" Helga cried.

"Wait here." He ran off, and she ripped frantically at the tape on her ankles. Then his headlights came probing, his door flung open, and she tumbled gratefully into the passenger seat. He handed her his gun, and rushed the Honda forwards, bumping over a weedy track that led to a country road.

Far ahead glowed the rear lights of the Mercedes; they vanished, then lit at another curve. Cursing, Selim gained, speeding like a racer. Biting her lips, Helga wrestled with her too-small harness, clicked it shut.

"Shoot out the tires," he urged, and she leaned out the window and fired wide. The Mercedes wobbled, accelerated.

She fired again and missed, but it swerved into an S-turn and skidded out, crashing through the barrier. Down a steep slope the Mercedes hurtled, side over side, smashing to a halt upside down. A fireball flared, reddening the darkness.

Selim screeched to a stop on the narrow shoulder. Lodged at the bottom of a ravine, the Mercedes was burning like a giant torch. Its doors didn't open. They stood side by side and watched it burn.

"Live by the sword," muttered Helga. "Die by the sword."

"Is that some German proverb?"

"I guess. Selim, you're the best partner in the world." She wrapped him in a bear hug and crushed him to her breast.

He started to laugh. "Let me go, please, Helga. I can't breathe."

"How did you ever find me, man?" She gave him a little shake.

"I couldn't give up our investigation. I was shadowing the Russians when they brought you in."

"We'd better call headquarters, and tell everybody how you saved my life."

Gazing down at the furious pyre he shivered: "The worst has been flashing back to my childhood."

"This is Germany. We've got rules and laws," Helga declared. "You're safe."

BURMA JUKEBOX

by SANFORD ALLEN

NO MATTER HOW PAUL TRIED TO POSITION HIMSELF on the too-soft, too-short bed, his back ached in a new place and the springs dug into his ass.

The way his feet hung off the end of the mattress, he felt like he was trying to bed down in a kids' playhouse.

The setting sun filtered through the motel's mildew green curtains, throwing a sickly light across the room. And a rust-colored stain on the yellowed lampshade made it look like a pair of skidmarked undies.

Even a Motel 6 with a caved-in roof would have been a step up from this, Paul thought as he fiddled with the TV remote. He wondered just how much shuteye he'd be getting tonight. He was exhausted, but he sure didn't see sleep coming easy at the E-Z Rest Motel.

The sign outside had promised free cable TV, but the circa-1985 set picked up all of four channels. The rest were like watching a snowstorm while listening to someone fry chicken.

Paul flipped between a car wax infomercial and CMT. It didn't take long to get bored of the infomercial. But the parade of slick-coiffed Nash-Vegas hucksters prancing around on the country music channel wasn't much better. They were playing some kind of cornball pop garbage that—aside from an occasional fiddle solo—wasn't anything like the country music he grew up on.

None of those hat tricks looked like they'd ever worked for a living, ever gotten dirt under their fingernails. Probably lived in Hollywood and drove BMWs.

Whatever happened to real, honest-to-God country music? Turned to shit just like everything else, Paul guessed.

He made another cycle through the channels, hoping that he'd missed one. Nope. The tube still picked up the same four.

When he got back to CMT, though, the picture started stretching to the side. It almost looked like it was melting off the screen.

The set's speaker made screechy sounds like a shortwave radio, and Paul heard some tinny, old-time country music with a steel guitar fade in. Seemed like an AM radio station was interfering with the signal or something.

"And that's the new one by Buck Owens," a DJ drawled over the final notes of the song. "Boy, ain't that one a goody. In news today, the Telstar satellite—"

There was a loud pop, then nothing but roaring static.

Paul clicked the off button and threw the remote down on the ugly floral-print comforter. What the hell was that all about? Everything about this dumpy motel was screwy as a soup sandwich.

Jesus, he had to get out of here.

The bedsprings let out a groan as Paul sat up and grabbed his boots. After today's repeated kicks in the teeth, he needed a beer. Needed one bad.

There had to be beer somewhere in the confines of Burma, New Mexico. The place was just a dust speck on the map, but there was no way his fate was bad enough that he'd break down in a town so tiny it didn't have at least one bar. What else, he wondered, did people do around here but drink?

Paul walked to the office. It smelled like incense and curry, neither of which he was fond of. The place was owned by an Indian couple who seemed nice enough, but he wondered how they ended up in Burma. Seemed like the place had to be a step down from just about everywhere, even some slum in Calcutta.

"Excuse me," he said to the owner, who was flipping through a stack of papers, eyeglasses propped at the end of his nose. "Know anyplace around here where a guy can get a beer?"

"Not here, sir," the man said, barely looking up from his work. "No hotel bar. One bar in this town only. Across the highway."

"How far is that? Walking distance?"

The man smiled and pushed up his glasses.

"Less than one mile. Your choice, sir, if that's too far to walk."

Paul nodded. He supposed he didn't have much choice but to hoof it.

At least the sun was almost gone as he set out. Things had started to cool off. Probably would get kind of chilly as night fell, he guessed. A little chilly air would feel pretty good after he'd had to hike three or four miles that afternoon in 100-degree heat.

His Chevy truck had broken down just after three in a flurry of steam and sputters. He left it on the side of the highway and started walking, desert sun beating on him like a red-hot hammer. By the time he made it to Burma, he was sopping with sweat and about ready to pass out.

The owner of the town's one truck stop, a grease-smeared slob named McCoy, dragged the car back with the town's one tow truck and pointed Paul to the town's one motel. McCoy also told him that the car needed a new radiator, which would set him back $450. And, oh yeah, it wouldn't be ready until tomorrow afternoon.

Christ, Paul thought, why couldn't I have broken down somewhere with more than a single stoplight? Maybe someplace near a Days Inn with a pool, maybe even a Denny's. Shit, he would even have settled for an Econo Lodge with an ice machine and a Waffle House across the parking lot.

Paul trudged down the road in the direction the hotel owner had pointed him. He looked out at the desolate landscape of rock and sand. What an ugly damn stretch of country. It was kind of like the surface of the moon, only with a few scrubby bushes stabbed into the ground every few yards. The sun had mostly disappeared by now, and the sky was the color of a bruise.

What kind of person, he wondered, wanted to live in a Godforsaken place like this? Seemed like everything around here was dead or well on its way to dying. He could only imagine how the loneliness would play with peoples' heads. Probably drove them all nuts.

He never would have ended up here if he hadn't gone out to California. He never should have made the trip. But his ex, Jill, had sounded so Goddamn desperate on the phone.

And he wanted to be a good father. For once.

Jill told him their daughter, Jen, was failing her junior year of high school, drinking, staying out all night. She'd discovered a pharmacy-worth of pills in Jen's purse. Their daughter needed to go into rehab, and Jill wanted Paul there for support.

So he drove to California. What else could he do?

The visit hadn't been easy. There were tears. There were denials. But Jen walked into the doors of the rehab place on her own free will. Paul felt hopeful about that much.

But it was driving Jill back to her apartment that made him regret the trip. She set in on him just like old times. Started accusing him of being an absentee father, blaming him for all their daughter's problems.

Things got worse when he told Jill that he wouldn't have been nearly so absentee a father if she hadn't up and moved to the West Coast, taking their daughter along. On the salary he earned fixing copy machines, it was awful hard to make it out to California more than once a year, especially with the amount of child support he paid each month.

Once things turned into a shouting match, Paul ordered Jill out of the car and headed directly back to Houston. Or he tried to anyway.

He'd mapped out the quickest route and made the mistake of getting off the big highways to save time. Didn't exactly work out that way.

Instead, he ended up broken down in Burma.

Hell, "Broken Down in Burma" sounded like a good cry-in-your-beer country song. He'd have to remember that. Sell it to George Jones or something.

Paul shook his head and continued down the road, dust clinging to his boots and jeans. He walked under the highway, hearing the rhythmic thud-thud of a tractor trailer passing overhead. On the other side of the overpass, there was a boarded up gas station, rusted-out pumps leaning at 45 degree angles.

In the sand behind it was what looked like a graveyard for old cars—a few dozen decaying hulks littering the landscape, tires and shredded seats scattered around them. A couple of newer cars were in there too. They seemed out-of-place, but Paul figured they'd probably shit their transmissions, burned out their motors, or something else too expensive to fix.

He thought about what happened to all the people who owned the cars. Did they hop the next Greyhound once their rides crapped out? Call someone to pick them up? He half wondered if they ended up buried in the desert while the slob who owned the truck stop stripped down their cars and pawned their belongings next town over.

Damn, that was right out of some kind of drive-in horror flick. The town was creeping him out, making him think all crazy.

As he cleared the car graveyard, Paul wondered if it had been a mile yet. Seemed like it had been at least that far. His feet were starting to ache, and the dust was sticking to his lips now, not just his boots. He spat and kept walking.

Finally, after he got to the top of a short incline, Paul saw the bar.

The place was a rectangular stone building with a porch in front. The porch railing looked to be made out of old wagon wheels. He could see a glow through the place's single window.

As Paul got closer, he read the little wooden sign on top of the building. "D&H TAVERN." In faded paint, it promised "COLD BEER, GREAT JUKEBOX."

There was a faint thump from inside that Paul chalked up to the "great jukebox." A couple of old neon beer signs hung in the window.

He smirked to himself as he checked out the brand names on the signs—Falstaff and Ballantine. He really was in the middle of Bumfuck, Egypt. Nobody drank Falstaff or Ballantine anymore, did they? Maybe in Burma. Time must stand still here.

The boards gave a little as Paul clattered his way to the front door. He guessed there weren't too many fat barflies around these parts. Anybody over 250 pounds would break right through the timbers.

He tugged open the door and stepped inside.

First thing he saw was a big Wurlitzer jukebox up against the wall, all chrome, glass and gaudy bands of green and red neon. Its Christmassy glow mingled with the light from the beer signs in the window.

Paul recognized the song. "Saginaw, Michigan" by Lefty Frizzell. Now there was a blast from the past. He remembered his granddad picking that tune on his old Gibson when the family would get together to barbecue and play dominoes.

The whole place looked straight out of a time warp. Not a thing in it could have been made after 1962.

The bar was the kind of chrome and Formica deal you'd see in a '50s diner. Same with the tables and booths. A faded tapestry of dogs playing poker hung above a pool table with worn, grey-green felt.

Standing behind the counter was an older man in a white western snap shirt with a couple of big red musical notes embroidered over the pockets. The guy's slicked-back silver hair and jug-handle ears made Paul think of Lyndon Baines Johnson.

"What can I do ya for?" the old-timer said as Paul walked to the bar, boot heels clicking on the scuffed linoleum floor. Looked like the guy was ready for some company. Poor bastard was probably bored out of his gourd.

"A cold one sounds awful good right now. What you got?"

"You name it, pardner. We got Bud, Miller, Schlitz, Ballantine's, Falstaff. Whatever you like."

Paul swung out a leg and dropped onto one of the padded barstools. Felt good to get off his feet after that walk.

"Never had a Falstaff before. Those pretty good?"

"I'd say so," the old guy said, smiling. He lifted an open Falstaff longneck from behind the bar. "Been my brand long as I been drinkin'."

"Well, I'll give it a try then. Must be good if you stuck with it that long."

The old guy nodded and slid open the refrigerator case behind the bar. He popped open a bottle and sat it on a cocktail napkin.

"You reckon you need a glass with that?"

"Save the glass for somebody else. I like mine right out of the bottle." Paul took a swig. The beer was cold. Any colder and there would have been ice crystals floating on top. After his ball-buster of a day in the New Mexico heat, it felt damned good going down.

The Lefty Frizzell song ended, and the jukebox made a few clicks and clacks as it changed records. It hissed as the needle dropped on a new one. Paul recognized the lazy, tinkling piano from "Crazy" by Patsy Cline.

"Boy," said Paul. "There's another classic."

The old guy smiled and nodded. "Don't reckon you'll find too many on my jukebox that ain't."

"That's quite a jukebox, too. All that neon and whatnot. They don't even make that kind anymore, do they?"

“No, I don’t reckon they do. All the new ones play them CDs now, from what they tell me.”

“Can you still get those little old 45 records like that thing plays?”

“Oh, I pick ‘em up, time to time. Got my sources. Never any new ones though. Just the oldies-but-goodies.”

Paul nodded. “How long you been here? This bar, I mean.”

“This fall it’ll be 45 years.”

“Is that right? So you’re either the D or the H in the name, I take it?”

“I’m the D. The H—well, Helga—she ain’t with us no longer.”

The old guy nodded to a yellowed photo of a woman that hung behind the bar. He raised his beer, nodded to the picture and took a swig.

Paul squinted to look at the photo. Helga had a big blonde hairsprayed mane to rival Tammy Wynette’s and a pair of black cat’s eye glasses. She wore a cowgirl outfit with a silky shirt and a red fringed vest. Looked like she was a real honky-tonk angel back in the day.

“I’m real sorry to hear that,” Paul said, extending his hand across the bar. “Looks like she was a pretty lady. I’m Paul, by the way.”

The old guy gripped his hand like a vice and shook it firmly. Old school. Not like the limp dishrags people took for handshakes these days.

“Name’s Dick. But some young fellers ain’t comfortable saying that. If you ain’t, you can just call me Richard.”

Paul laughed.

“I think I’m OK with calling you Dick. Doesn’t bother me too much.” He took a pull off of his beer. “Doesn’t seem like you get much business around here, Dick.”

“Nah. Not much of a town here no more. Over the years, people up and moved to places where there was better jobs and better times. I just keep coming in here to have something to do. Done paid off the building a long time ago, and I sell enough beer to keep the lights on.” He shrugged. “I got all them old records to keep me company, and I always got a cold one at arm’s reach.”

“Sounds like life’s not too bad.”

“Nah. Little lonely at times, real lonely some others, but I can’t rightly complain, all considered."

Paul took another drink of his Falstaff. It sure felt good to unwind with a cold one after everything that had happened. And for some reason, he liked talking to the old codger. Just shooting the breeze with someone calm and sensible helped take his mind off all the crazy things that had happened.

"All those old records bring back some memories, I bet."

"Yup," Dick said. "I kindly remember differ'nt people by 'em is how it works. Like that one, 'Crazy.' I got that one after some lady come through here kind of broke up and cryin' about a guy done her wrong. She sat there on that exact barstool, cried her heart out to me. I done my duty as bartender to keep 'em coming and let her tell her story. She said she was crazy for lovin' a feller kept doing her wrong. Made me think of that ol' tune."

The Patsy Cline ended, and there were a few clicks as the Wurlitzer changed records again. A new single dropped in place, and Paul heard the opening bars of "Branded Man" by Merle Haggard.

"That one right there," Dick said, nodding to the jukebox. "That one's a whole differ'nt story. Old feller come in here, just got outta the pen. He's traveling to see his daughter first time since he got out. Think he told me he was in for 30-some years. Armed robbery gone wrong. He told me he just wasn't sure what life would be like after he's branded a convict."

"So you put that record on the jukebox in his honor?"

"Something like that. People come in, and if they got something interesting to say, well, I get me a record I can keep around to remind me of 'em."

Paul drained his bottle and put it down.

"Another one, Paul?"

"Sure, put it on my tab."

Dick reached into the cooler case, uncapped a longneck and set it on the counter on top of a fresh napkin.

"Reckon you're just passin' through. Like the rest."

"Yeah. Visited the ex out in California," Paul said lifting a finger and making the 'crazy' sign by his temple. "Damn truck broke down on the way back. They're fixing it over at the truck stop."

He took a long pull of the beer.

"Happens time to time," Dick said.

“Say,” Paul said jerking his thumb in the direction of the car graveyard he passed along the way. “What’s up with all those rusted out cars over there? Used car lot gone to pot or something?”

Dick chuckled, his paunch jiggling over his silver belt buckle.

“Nah. Mostly just old cars that gived up the ghost along the highway. Just kind of piled up over the years.”

“Yeah, I guess the heat’s murder on a car. I found that out myself the hard way.” Paul shook his head and wiped some condensation from the beer bottle with his thumb.

“Fitting way to end up the trip, I guess, bad as the whole thing was going. Had to go out there to put my daughter in rehab, then the ex sets in on me with all sorts of guilt tripping and crazy talk. Ended up a hell of a fight. Figured I had one more kick in the balls coming before it was all over. They come in threes.”

“Yup. Sometimes it sure seems that way.”

Paul nodded and looked down at his beer.

“You try to do what’s right, you know. Isn’t always so easy. I always paid my child support. Did what I could for my girl considering she and her mama were on the other side of the country. Guess I wonder if I could have moved out there. Maybe tried to do more.”

The older man shrugged. “Sounds like there’s been heartaches all around,” he said. “Plenty of ‘em. Yours, your ex’s, your girl’s.”

Paul nodded. “Yeah. I suppose I’ve got some, and I suppose I’ve probably caused my share. Thing is, I miss my girl, and I sometimes I even miss her crazy mama.”

“Well, alls you can do is rest behind knowing you did what you could. Ain’t no amount of wonderin’ gonna make things different from how they turned out. How’s that old song go? ‘Ev’ry hour through the day since you’ve been away, I keep wonderin’.’ Webb Pierce done that one.”

“See,” Paul said, tapping his finger on the bar. “That’s why those old songs on your jukebox are better than that new, Nash-Vegas crap. They’re about real people with real problems. You can relate to them.”

“Yessir. I surely think there’s a good ol’ country song for just about any heartbreak a man could experience. Another beer?”

“Yeah, I figure I’m not driving. Why not?”

Dick sat another Falstaff down on the counter.

"Didn't even know you could get these anymore. Falstaffs, I mean."

"Yup. Distributor reckons I'm about the only place around here still buys 'em."

"Well, I'm glad I got to try it. Not a bad beer."

"Like I said, it's been my brand for a good long while."

Paul took one swig, then another. He'd have to look for Falstaff down at the Randall's near his house. Didn't taste half bad at all. Kind of fit with the old honky-tonk music on the jukebox, in fact.

"Well, it's cold enough to make me forget the heat, and it's doing its job making me forget all the problems I got stacked up."

"Yup. That's why beer got invented, I reckon."

Dick took a swig and looked up at the picture of Helga behind the bar. The two men sat for a while and listened as the jukebox rang out its hit parade from decades long gone—"One Woman Man" by Johnny Horton, "He'll Have to Go" by Jim Reeves, "Walking the Floor Over You" by Ernest Tubb.

After a couple more tunes played through, Paul drained his bottle and put it down on the bar napkin. A few more brews would hit the spot, but he had a mile to go in the dark. Probably better to do it walking than stumbling.

"Well, Dick. It's been a pleasure talking to you. How much I owe you for those beers?"

"Oh, don't worry about them beers, pardner. The pleasure's been all mine."

"You sure?"

"Sure as shittin'."

As Paul pulled himself up off of the barstool, the older man turned to the cash register. He punched a key and the "No Sale" flag popped up.

A loud "ka-ching" rang through the bar, and the jukebox lost power for just a second. Its lights blinked and the needle lifted up before the end of the "Oh, Lonesome Me" by Don Gibson.

Silence.

◊◊◊◊◊

Dick turned to see the barstool was no longer occupied. He smiled, satisfied, sipped from his Falstaff and put it back down.

He walked out from behind the bar. There, sitting on the stool where the younger man had been, was a 45 record in a yellowed paper sleeve.

The old man picked up the record and laid it carefully on the Formica bar top.

He walked back to his phone and dialed.

"McCoy, this here's Dick. That truck come in today? You can take what you need off it, drop it down with others. Looks like we got another one that's stickin' around."

He listened for a bit.

"Yep. You have a good one too, hear? And tell the missus I said 'Howdy.'"

He put the receiver back in place, then picked up the 45 and examined its bright orange label. "Heartaches by the Numbers" by Ray Price.

"Now there's one I ain't heard in a spell," the old man said. "Reckon that will go real good on the jukebox. Nice of you to stop in, Paul."

LEPERS

by Keyan Bowes

EYES AVERTED, VIJAY HURRIES PAST THE GROUP OF LEPERS clustered round a small trash-fire on the sidewalk. Bombay has so many, with horrifying gargoyle faces and missing toes. The neon street lamps cast a dim purplish light on uneven cobbled sidewalks lined with the cocoon-like figures of sleeping street dwellers.

It's after 2 a.m., and the last train has left. The gothic bulk of Victoria Terminus rises before him, its ominous carvings peering into the dark through hundreds of eyes. The air smells of feces, night-scented flowers, the sea, and a rotting rat. There's no taxi anywhere.

"Bhai?" says a voice. "Brother?"

A man steps from the shadows. His nose is gone, and a hole gapes in one cheek. Vijay walks on quickly, suppressing pity and disgust. Leprosy. In the wealthy, it's Hansen's disease; the victims get treated and recover. The poor get crippled and beg.

"Bhai?" The man stumbles along behind him. "Vijay-bhai? Don't you recognize me?"

As the leper speaks, he does.

"Raj? What…? They told me you were dead. Two years ago. In the April of 1975…" Raj. Vijay's childhood friend. Raj, who died while Vijay was studying overseas, and Vijay had wept secretly over Mother's letter.

"Yes," Raj says, his voice soft and harsh, his eyes shadowed by the dirty shawl wrapping him. "I'm dead."

"Don't say that!" In a flash, Vijay understands. Raj didn't die, he contracted the living death of leprosy. Mother's letter lied, to save him pain and Raj's family shame.

"They can cure leprosy nowadays," Vijay says. Why hadn't his family done something? Money problems, most likely. "They have medicines. Don't worry about the cost. Tomorrow, I myself will take you…"

Raj interrupts him. "This is not leprosy, Vijay-bhai. No hospital will help me."

It's true that Raj looks terrible, much worse than any of the other lepers. "Of course, they will help you," Vijay says. "If it isn't leprosy, then the doctors will find out what it is." Yaws? Kala-azar? Something.

Raj just shakes his head no.

Damn this fatalism! He must get him to treatment. Maybe his family actually tried, maybe Raj just refused.

"Vijay, I truly am dead," Raj says. "I have no breath."

"What?" Vijay says, trying to reason with him. "If you were dead, you would be cremated!"

"My body disappeared from the hospital before my family arrived. I am dead. *Mein hoon ek zinda laash.*"

Zinda laash. A living corpse. A zombie. Suddenly, Vijay's terrified.

The Raj-creature steps into the hard light beneath a street lamp, and pulls a long knife from under his shawl. Vijay jumps back, ready to run.

"A tantric promised he could make me wealthy, pay for my sister's wedding…he used me for his magic, killed me, turned me loose like this."

"But, what are you doing here?" Vijay asks warily, watching the knife. With the lepers, he means, but he doesn't say it. Raj seems to understand anyway.

"Where else would I go? When there is no hope, when you are a corpse who cannot die, even the ordinary street dwellers run away. The leper folk…understand."

Painfully, Raj bends down, places the knife on the ground. Most of his fingers are gone. The dark skin on his forearm is shriveled and ragged. "I stole this from a shop."

He struggles to his feet and removes the shawl, exposes a bare neck. "I waited two years for someone to help me. There is no one, only you…please kill me again."

Vijay swallows hard and picks up the knife with his handkerchief. A ripe smell of decay overlays the scents of feces and flowers and the sea. He tries to steel himself for what he has to do.

Someone coughs. The group of beggars is watching him, heads turn from the fire. Vijay looks at them, at the knife, at Raj. He hears a quiet voice from among them. "Kill me too, sir…"

"I can't!" Vijay cries and steps back. "Raj, I promise I'll arrange your sister's wedding." And he drops the knife with a clatter.

The lepers murmur. Vijay walks away hurriedly, trying not to run. "Sahib!" someone calls. It's not Raj. "*O, kayar-sahib!*" Hey, Sir Coward. Vijay turns back to see a leper lifting the knife, using both stump-fingered hands. As he watches, the man hacks at Raj's neck until the head falls to the paving stones with a fleshy thud, and the body collapses into a pile of rags. The warm stench of decay overpowers all the other smells. The executioner looks at him, his eyes dark pits under the harsh street lamp.

The leper's had the guts to do what he couldn't.

Vijay pauses, salutes him. The man gives a small nod and returns to the fire. Vijay continues his lonely walk. Sir Coward indeed. The sea wind is blowing in his eyes. Maybe that's what's making them water.

THE DEEP END

by JAKE BURROWS

THE HUMIDITY KILLED HIS IPOD JUST AS THE EDITORS were lamenting the sadness of "Smokers Outside a Hospital Room." This left Perry victim to the tinny strains of Tricia Yearwood struggling to escape the broken and buzzing speakers of the aging bus. The heat plastered him to the cracked vinyl, his discomfort made worse by the collective carbon dioxide emissions of a dozen or so passengers joining him on the rural route. It smelled like late night Waffle House: bacon, grits, and the sulfur of undercooked eggs.

The bus squealed to a halt and the driver announced "Homerville Falls." Perry grabbed his backpack and squeezed off. The absence of a breeze provided no respite as he shouldered his pack and headed towards the outskirts of town, but he was happy to be free from the perspiring flesh and noxious diesel.

He hiked down the worn country road, surrounded by thick kudzu that seemed to consume the forest edge. Passing a boiled peanut stand, he wondered what in the hell a boiled peanut tasted like and why anyone would boil a peanut in the first place. There were no clues given, neither by the rusty and tarnished cooking implements that apparently were used in the process, nor by the slack-jawed tween whose daisy-dukes and tube top were overflowing with adolescent corpulence.

The noisy chorus of insects ebbed and pulsed as Perry reflected on the 1,500-plus mile journey that was nearing its end. It was less than a month ago that his dying father coughed out the revelation that Perry's grandmother was still alive—a fact made shocking by a lifetime of lies to the contrary.

"Alive and in Georgia." His father had managed.

After falling back into unconsciousness, his father later awoke with a series of other revelations that explained and perhaps justified his previous deceptions. Perry's grandmother had spent her life as a whore and a drug addict. She had bounced around as a member of several religious cults. She had been arrested for selling counterfeit food stamps, and perhaps worse, had attempted to recruit her family and friends into Amway.

Be it the morphine or a dying man's guilt, Perry's father asked him to find the woman and inform her of his death. No apologies, no explanations, just a simple announcement:

"Your son is dead."

The sign for the Eternity Pond Trailer park looked about three decades old and in need of fresh paint. Perry followed the dirt road beyond the sign until it opened up in a massive forested clearing. The kudzu was especially thick here and all but blotted out the sunlight, shrouding the scores of dilapidated mobile homes in an oppressive gloom.

As he entered the trailer park, Perry noted a line of old tables covered with assorted backpacks, purses, shoes, and clothes. A rough "For Sale" sign was taped to the front of the table.

The park was set up in a rough semicircle surrounding an algae-covered pond, which was presumably its namesake. Rows of chairs representing a myriad of shapes and styles were set in seeming semi-permanence around the edge of the pond.

It was obvious that little effort was made in the park's upkeep and if it were not for the occasional sign of human movement, Perry would have assumed the park was abandoned.

Perry had found his grandmother's address through a simple online search, but none of the trailers were conspicuously marked. He approached an elderly man who was staring fixedly into the darkness of the pond.

As he drew closer, Perry was halted in his tracks by the unclean stench of the old man's body. It was as if he hadn't bathed since the park was founded. Gagging slightly, Perry tried to get the man's attention.

"Excuse…excuse me sir?" he said.

The man slowly turned and gave Perry a wide toothless grin. There was something wrong with him, something that was difficult for Perry to pinpoint. His eyes were a bit too bright. His skin was too smooth and youthful. It was as if a young man were trying to masquerade as an old one.

"Deeper than you can imagine, young man," he rasped absently.

Perry tried to clear the thickness from his throat and asked for Nora Ramsay's trailer. He was surprised when the man immediately pointed to a lime green trailer not far from where they stood. Perry thanked him and went to meet his grandmother. He had assumed that she had since died and his task would have ended here.

At this point he almost wished that it were the case.

He approached the singlewide mobile home. It was rooted in thick weeds and the structure was shedding its aluminum siding like a snake sloughs off its skin.

How could anyone live in these conditions?

His sole desire was to deliver his message quickly and then jump on the Amtrak back to Vermont. With trepidation, he rapped on the trailer's flimsy door.

A few minutes later, the door opened, assailing him with the gut-wrenching smell of food long gone bad.

His grandmother stood there, a blank look upon her smooth face. The resemblance to his father was unmistakable, and her hair was the same ginger color as his own—surprisingly showing no sign of graying. She wore a dingy white t-shirt that said "God Accepts Knee-mail" that was covered with a rainbow array of dubious stains.

"Ms. Ramsay?" he asked.

Her bright eyes opened wider.

"Yes," she replied. "I suppose that's me."

And he poured out the story; his father's lung cancer, his dying words, and the 1,500-plus mile trip from Killington. As an addendum, Perry indicated his need to get back on the road very soon.

"Nonsense," she said. "You must stay a while. You are family after all. We must…reconnect."

Perry was stricken by the far away sound of her voice. She sounded heavily medicated.

In this moment he wanted to be anywhere but here. The remoteness of the location, combined with the oppressive humidity, the decrepit state of the park and the sour odor of its inhabitants left him feeling as if he was mired in a bad dream. The surrealism created a pervasive sense of disassociation.

But then there was his father, laying there dying, drowning in his own fluids. His father, who did his best for him, bought him his first guitar, paid for the lessons, went to every show. His father, who had one simple request before he died. His grandmother stepped aside, and Perry held his breath and entered the trailer.

It was worse than he could imagine. The smell of rotting food was combined with the repugnant odor of human waste and animal decomposition. Perry immediately keeled over and noisily lost his lunch on the linoleum tile. He did his best to steady himself but failed, his outstretched hand stiff-arming the floor and planting in the remains of a putrefied cat.

Perry looked at the cat, then looked at his hand and felt his world slip away from him. He made a half-hearted turn back towards the door but his legs failed him. Instead, he collapsed to the stained floor; his sight plunged into a fitful darkness.

It must have only been a few seconds and Perry's vision returned to him with horrible clarity. His grandmother, who was otherwise completely unfazed about the whole ordeal, was holding a murky glass of liquid in front of his face.

"This will make you right as rain," she said with the same distant effect as before.

Perry got up on his hands and knees and crawled his way towards a brown plaid loveseat.

God accepts knee-mail, he thought as he fought his nausea to make it to the loveseat.

Once seated, Perry was better able to survey the trailer around him. While his grandmother stood motionless with the glass of liquid still outstretched in front of her, Perry looked around.

"This will make you right as rain," she repeated.

The trailer had not been cleaned in years. According to the faded calendar on the wall it was still October 1987, and the coffee pot had since been taken over by blue-green mold. Next to it, a (presumably) basket of fruit had disintegrated into a multi-colored, viscous gel. Perry could make out the rough shape of a banana, but the rest was a mystery. It was the land that time forgot.

And still she stood there with a stupid grin on her face and the outstretched glass of murky water.

"Right as rain," she said.

And those bright, bright eyes...

Oddly, the entire kitchen and dining area were filled with glasses, containers, tubs, buckets, and a host of other conveyances, some of which still contained the same murky liquid that sloshed in Perry's face and promised a cure for what ailed him.

Whatever it was that would make him "right as rain" looked like it had been doing so for his grandmother for some time.

"I'm not thirsty," he said, and rubbed his eyes. "Sorry about your floor."

His grandmother's face twisted into exaggerated disappointment.

"Not thirsty?" she croaked.

"Your son, my father is dead," he said. "Don't you have anything to say about that? I mean, don't you care?"

A moment of cognition seemed to flash in her eyes as if some part of her addled brain were considering the impact of his questions. She smiled at him earnestly, revealing a badly stained set of dentures.

"We were not close, your father and I," she said, choosing her words carefully. "He did not always approve of my...lifestyle. It's been so long though. So very long."

Perry steeled himself to stand. He had done what he had come here to do, and he needed to escape the filthy confines of his grandmother's trailer home.

"Please," she said, "don't leave yet. Sometimes we celebrate."

"Who celebrates?" asked Perry.

"We do. The park. My neighbors."

"I don't want...look, thank you anyway, but..." Perry stood to leave, but his grandmother's face took on a pitiful visage.

"But you're all the family I have left," she whimpered.

Perry sighed and fought back the urge to vomit again.

◊◊◊◊◊

The trailer park was illuminated by a seemingly impossible number of Citronella tiki torches, bathing the pond in a flickering orange glow. Each of the park's one hundred and fifty elderly residents had brought their own, stabbing it mechanically in the soft earth just beyond the rows of chairs.

Each went back to their homes and returned with empty buckets, bottles, plastic tubs, and Tupperware containers. They then dutifully sat down in a chair of their apparent choosing.

Perry watched this, bemused, tugging from an old bottle of Jim Beam his grandmother had graciously provided. She stood beside him conspicuously vibrating with excitement.

"It will be quite extraordinary, you'll see," she chattered.

At this point he could give a shit. His earlier trepidation had since been replaced by a bourbon-fueled ambivalence. He had resolved to stay the night. He'd camp outside near the pond and then leave in the morning. Whatever this "celebration" was about it was important to his grandmother, and his acquiescence was a small matter in the face of his father's death.

A karmic deposit, he thought.

A crooked armature of a man joined them, a bright red fez sat on his head sporting a wide assortment of buttons, pins, and ribbons.

His grandmother, full of deference, introduced him has Walt Kalinsky, the president of the trailer park association. Walt's eyes were wide and bright and threatened to pop out of his skull while his dentures rattled in his mouth like a Yahtzee cup before the roll. He carried a leather-bound book in one hand and an empty gallon jug in the other.

And his hands were unusually smooth, Perry noticed.

Walt motioned for Perry and his grandmother to step forward to the edge of the pond.

"Esteemed Eternity Pond residents," said Walt, "our dear neighbor Nora has brought us the pleasure of her grandson's presence."

The crowd applauded politely.

"I would like to take this opportunity to welcome him to our community." Walt paused.

The crowd suddenly filled with a series of murmured "welcomes."

"In accordance with the bylaws of the Eternity Pond Trailer Park Association, we will now invite Mr. Perry Ramsay to become an honorary member of our community."

Perry slugged back another gulp of Jim Beam and smiled and nodded to the crowd. His grandmother leaned in and whispered:

"We have a silly little custom here." She said. "When we invite you into our community we ask that you take a dip in the pond."

"The pond? Nah, I'm all set." Perry replied.

He noticed that all eyes were on him. His grandmother had taken on that disappointed look, and Walt gave him an embarrassed smile and then apologized to the crowd with his eyes.

"Just a little dip?" His grandmother implored. "It would mean so much to me."

Perry looked around at the crowd. Walt's bug eyes stared at him expectantly. His grandmother had adopted the same hurt look as before, and the crowd was waiting for something to happen.

It was, perhaps, the sheer embarrassment of the situation that caused him to move.

"What the fuck." He shrugged, and kicked off his shoes. After taking another swig of the Beam, Perry peeled off his shirt and socks and stepped into the pond.

It was like bathwater—warm from the Georgia sun and not at all unpleasant.

Perry decided to make a show of it and dove into the murky water and began an exaggerated, if not clumsy, butterfly stroke. The crowd cheered, his grandmother beamed, and Walt nodded approvingly.

He'd become a part of their community, make his grandmother happy, and in doing so bridge a twenty-year gap between his father and her. Everyone deserved forgiveness, even his drug-abusing, Amway-distributing, whore of a grandmother.

It was probably Mr. Beam talking, but Perry felt absolutely elated. He had his reservations at first, but the feel of the fresh water on his skin enlivened him. He swam harder towards the far end.

Deeper than you can imagine…

Maybe it was the bourbon, or perhaps the two weeks of traveling, but Perry's endurance began to give on him. Just how deep was this pond anyway?

In a panic, he stopped swimming aggressively and stretched his feet towards the pond's muddy bottom.

Nothing.

He then noticed for the first time that Walt had begun reading from the leather-bound book.

"...belu, en haptu belu. En amreke val n'bia..."

Perry, treading water, looked around at the crowd and saw a predatory look upon their faces.

"...belu, en haptu belu. En amreke val n'bia!!!"

Walt's voice had become something else, something much more sinister.

But Perry didn't have time to focus on that, for the water below his feet began to move and churn as if a school of carp were darting in an out of his legs.

"Grandma!" He yelled, the tone of his voice betraying his fear. He felt like a toddler, a child, and his pleas were met with the wild-eyed looks of the spectators around him.

The orange-hued water around hum began to bubble with the activity of movement below.

The crowd rose from their chairs and approached the water, their eyes wide and bright and full of an unnatural hunger.

Perry swam towards the bank, but it seemed so far away to him and his body felt so heavy. He floundered in the water gasping for air and struggling to stay afloat.

Deeper than you can imagine...

Suddenly, the light from the torches reflected off of something slick and glistening that broke the surface. In the moment that he saw it, Perry could make out a mottled salmon-colored appendage.

Perry gasped, and the crowd grunted with satisfaction. He glanced up and saw them eagerly race towards the water, their arms full of empty jugs and containers. They moved with the energy and vitality of people a quarter their apparent age.

"No pushing!" yelled Walt. "There will be plenty for everyone."

Plenty? Perry thought. Plenty of what?

Something firm and unyielding wrapped around his feet and squeezed with enormous strength. Without the ability to tread water, Perry panicked and thrashed at the darkness around him. The crowd responded with excitement, their grunts and cries reaching frenzied levels.

"Oh God!" he screamed. "Oh God, oh God, oh God!"

The fetid water filled his mouth as quickly as he could spit it out. The appendage that pinned his legs began to cut into his flesh and pull him under. The pain flashed in an instance, reached maximum intensity, and then left him numb.

The water around him filled with his blood, black in the torchlight. Completely helpless to resist, Perry screamed until his lungs filled with water.

As the thing in the pond pulled his flailing body beneath the surface, the last image to register were scores of fanatical trailer park residents filling their containers with the blood-tainted pond water. His grandmother, though, lacked the patience.

She rested on all fours, her face planted in the water gulping thirstily.

Feeling right as rain…

MIKE (MY SECOND ROOMMATE)

by ADAM ARMOUR

THERE WAS A DROP OF RED ON THE FLOOR; A SMALL DARK spot on the otherwise flawless off-white carpet spread throughout our apartment, and I just knew it was blood.

I hovered on my haunches and stared down at the spot, took my finger and touched it to the stain and then to my tongue just like they do in the movies, but since I didn't really know what blood tasted like, it didn't help. Regardless, it was a stain and I was pissed.

Clenching my teeth, I looked toward the closed bedroom door of my new roommate, Mike.

"What about the deposit, you idiot," I mumbled. "What about the deposit?"

But, instead of complaining like I had every right to do, I let it go with a sigh, stood and went to my room and shut the door. Mike and I had to get along. This wasn't about to be another Sam situation.

Tell the truth, I was pretty thrilled when Mike answered my ad. I'd never met a movie star before, and he used to be a pretty big one. You've probably seen some of his comedies.

"I caught your last movie on satellite," I told him during his interview. "It was pretty decent." And he just nodded quietly the way he always does, that pale mask he never seems to remove revealing nothing.

I chalked it up to the eccentricities of celebrity. I've seen those television shows about famous people in rehab, publicly working out all their bizzaro problems. I figured Mike was much the same.

So, he didn't really talk or interact at all, consistently wore this outfit consisting of a creepy mask and jumpsuit, came dragging in at all hours of the night and occasionally tracked droplets of blood into our home? I still sleep with a stuffed animal. We all got our ticks.

Take, for instance, Sam. He was nothing but a ball of eccentricity, all long hair and pompous attitude, ranting and raving about how he was smarter than his philosophy professor and how he was taking Japanese so that he could better understand the intricacies of anime. He also watched a lot of art flicks, which I hated: foreign language coming-of-age stories and low budget black-and-white shit with lots of talk and little happening. Worst part was he always wanted me to hang out with him and never understood why I didn't. I spent my free time shut in my room, playing video games or reading while he'd go out and do stuff—attend film screenings in this tiny room at the top of the student union or go out and eat Greek or Thai. I was invited, but I'd never go. Never really wanted to, either. I liked to be alone. Nothing wrong with that, right?

Wrong, I suppose, as it was a real sore point between the two of us, right up until I'd had enough of him.

But, I just knew things with Mike were going to be different, that the two of us were going to get along exceptionally well. First off, he never said anything, which meant I never had to listen to him ramble on and on endlessly about teachers being pretentious assholes or scream the word "fuck" eight times in a row at bleed-through-walls volume about how his computer doesn't work right even though he was the idiot who didn't know how the "insert" key functioned. Instead of ranting, Mike did a lot of quiet staring—hours spent in silence in one corner of our small apartment, staring out at nothing in particular. It was great.

But then, two weeks into what I considered to be a very symbiotic relationship, I found the blood on the floor. The next night, he brought home his first girl. She was a brunette, I think, though it was hard to tell with all that dried blood matting her hair and the arrow sticking out of her face.

Mike, of course, assumed I hadn't seen him dragging the body into the house so late. But, I'm a frequent pee-er, so I was just closing the door to my room after my usual 3 A.M. piss when he happened to walk in, pulling this chick's corpse behind him like a caveman in one of those cartoons. Through my cracked bedroom door I watched as he hauled her to his room and shut the door, and through the paper thin walls of our apartment I could hear him shoving her body in his closet and, afterwards, the groaning of his bed as it bore his heavy weight.

The next morning Mike was gone, so I sneaked into his room and opened the closet, just to see. Her one remaining eye was wide open, which was kind of creepy, and she stared out just beyond my head at the wall behind me kind of like Mike does from his corner of the living room. I wondered who she was and what classes she had been taking or why Mike decided to bring her here instead of dumping her body in a lake or something, like in the mafia flicks. In the end, I guess I figured maybe Mike was too busy making movies to be watching them all the time, unlike my last roommate. All he did was goof off.

Sam didn't even have a job; his parents paid his portion of the rent and half our utilities and gave him extra spending money to waste on his artsy movies and foreign lunches. I shoveled popcorn into tubs and then tubs into the hands of fatty moviegoers and obnoxious teens at the local theater every weekend in order to pay my portion of the rent. Sometimes I'd see Sam there with some of his pretentious asshole buddies, if we had some subtitled German indie flick on one of the small screens. He'd come to the counter and ask "What's up?" and then buy a pack of Twizzlers or something and I'd just look at him and not even say anything. And he still had the balls to ask why I never hung out on the weekends.

But Mike was cool. He never did any shit like that. I mean, I don't know what the hell he did on the weekends because I was never there, and he never brought any of the girls he murdered to the movies or anything; but he also never gave me guff about working to pay the bills. Thank God.

But, you know, despite the fact that Mike was famous and didn't irritate the shit out of me like Sam, I began to have a real problem with his messy hobby. There's only so much eccentricity a guy can take, after all. Over the next few weeks, Mike began to drag more and more bodies into his room, all young girls—brunettes, blonds and redheads alike; he didn't seem to have a preference—all hacked to pieces or brutally slain with some manner of home care or sporting equipment. And little droplets of blood began spotting all over the damn carpet and although I scrubbed on my hands and knees with cold water and everything I just couldn't get them up and it pissed me off because I knew we weren't ever going to get that $500 deposit back. It wasn't long before the neighbors started complaining about the smell and, frankly they had every right to do so because our apartment was fairly ripe.

Although I never saw them for myself, the bodies must have really begun piling up in Mike's room because soon he was cramming them in the hallway closet too, though he still never said anything about it. Despite the fact that I could no longer sit comfortably in the living room without having to neutralize a sizable army of buzzing flies or that once the closet door hadn't closed completely because clearly, clearly there was a person's hand caught in it and as I walked by I said as loudly and clearly as possible "Geez, I wonder what this is coming out of the hallway closet. It looks like fingers. Oh, well," Mike still didn't say word one about it. I was beginning to think that maybe Sam hadn't been so bad after all. I mean, sure he was overbearing and annoying and had awful taste in movies, but at least I didn't have to deal with all this—with terrible stench, calls from the super, and blood all over the carpet.

I decided to confront Mike, tell him I didn't care how famous he was or how funny his last movie might have been, there's only so many bodies a guy can tolerate having in his closet before he just has to put up the octagonal sign, you know. So, late one night, as Mike desperately struggled to stuff some body parts in the small hallway closet already filled with too many, I just stepped from my room and said, "Okay, I've had e-freaking-nough of this."

Although the pale mask he always wore gave him an everlasting visage of impassivity, I imagine I must have surprised Mike because he dropped all the girl's pieces to the floor. It was then I had an epiphany. Mike just looked so pathetic standing there, jumpsuit covered in blood as he scrambled to pick up the body parts, and you know, I couldn't help but think that maybe I was the roommate with the problem, not Mike or Sam. Maybe if I had tried a little harder last time, Sam and I would still be on speaking terms. I mean, would it have killed me to sit through one movie?

And maybe Mike was just crying out for help. I mean, he was obviously slumming it somewhat by hanging out with a guy like me instead of all those Hollywood types. Maybe he just needed someone to understand that he had a thing, or a problem, or whatever, and just wanted somebody to understand him, someone who wasn't a tinsel town phony who wore a different kind of mask. He could have just been reaching out to someone real—to me—and instead of reaching back I just shut myself in my room like I always did, closing myself off from someone who needed a friend. I've always worried that maybe I'm not the person I should be, that maybe if I was a little more outgoing and not so aloof all the time that I'd be happier overall and not worry so much about the little things.

So, I sucked it up, decided it was time for a change.

"Here," I said, "Let me give you a hand with that." And I took my place next to my second roommate, Mike, who nodded at me appreciatively as I helped him push that girl's body into the closet, her warm blood running down my arm before falling, drop by drop, to the off-white carpet below.

The Invisible Tourists

by Kristine Ong Muslim

Gliding in and out
of our bodies,
the tourists regard us
with curiosity.

They sometimes
walk with us,
sloughing their grisly
remains across

the city streets,
but most of them
remain content
in watching.

In death, we will
understand them;
they will shed their skins
to make us believe

to make us remember
to make us understand
that we are so much
like them inside.

In Jack's Time

by Kristine Ong Muslim

It was the day the house had
changed to accommodate him.

The mirrors imploded
to banish his image forever.
The drapes assumed
the color of his freckled skin.

The light fixtures blinked
at the rate of his disappearing
childhood memories wrought
in gradations of light and dark.

In the living room, the grandfather
clock reduced time into physical
increments, because building
empty houses took time.

The bed linens turned into the same
silk that lined his ancestors' coffins.
The frozen roses of their shriveled
heads lay side by side on the freezer.

Now, every thing in the house
reeked of health and malice.
Even the whitewashed walls
gurgled secretly in their bones.

He heard his throat offer itself
to be opened up so that the god
that had been smothered inside
could peer out, rebuild the house.

Resurrection of a Paper Doll Cutout

by Kristine Ong Muslim

I pluck it free from the throes of the bloodbath,
scissor on the perforated lines where its paper-flesh
meets the world. It complains of tinnitus, tooth decay.

I cut out a belly button from a sheet of baby's skin, lick it,
stick it in place. She says she does not want it. I tell her
that all real girls have belly buttons. She finally agrees.

I curl her lashes. She blinks her eyes for the first time.
The fingers of her phantom limbs hide inside the drawer wher
I keep my socks. They twitch while she paints her nails red.

Èinstèin Rode Bìtch

by Brian Anglin

THE IDEA CAME TO ME THE SAME WAY ANY BREAKTHROUGH comes to a man of genius. I was drunk, and I was trying to get laid.

Of course, I was expecting it. I had worked out the formula for creativity as a pimple-faced teenager. Home alone, inebriated, and pining away for Elsie Wycoski, my teenage angst became numbers. Turns out the key to creativity is a very simple algebraic equation. It looks like this:

$E = mc^2$

Where:

m = Your level of sexual desperation

c = Your level of inebriation

E = Your level of creativity

In other words, the more desperate and drunk you are, the harder your brain works to come up with witty, clever things to say or do in order to get the girl sitting next to you back to your place and in the sack.

Okay, okay, I know some of you out there are screaming plagiarism and theft of intellectual property rights. Well, for those of you on the left side of the bell curve, I'm perfectly aware of Einstein's frequently misunderstood theory of energy and matter. But Einstein's equation is very different. His looks like this:

$E = mc^2$

Or, as Einstein hypothesized, energy equals the mass of an object times the speed of light squared. What a bunch of phooey!

Do you see the difference? Mine unlocks a mystery of the universe. His is a nebulous collision of numbers and words. Its only claim to fame is that it unwittingly inspired my own formula.

It's sad, actually. Having spent some time analyzing Einstein's scientific and personal writings, I'm pretty sure he had no idea how close he was to coming up with a really great idea and achieving intellectual immortality. If he'd had any understanding of the real meaning and application of his theory, he might have been more successful in his exploration of perpetual motion and cold fusion.

My guess is he got laid too much.

You see, once you understand the basic principals of $E=mc^2$, understanding condensed matter nuclear science is obvious. The secret to creating tremendous amounts of energy from matter without an atomic explosion is liquor and longing. It's a scientific fact that proves itself every Friday night. The drunker you get, the less likely you are to actually get laid. That, of course, results in increased levels of sexual desperation, which leads to more drinking. The unavoidable conclusion is that the two elements naturally and effortlessly fuel each other in a perpetual cycle. As a result, there is a tremendous explosion of energy—creative energy.

Now that we all have a fundamental understanding of how the universe works, it should come as no surprise that as one of the world's leading minds in the field of temporal physics and macrobiotic biochemical artificial intelligence, I seek out beer and rejection every chance I get.

Last Friday was no different.

Looking around the table, I saw the usual circle of faces. There were science geeks, neo-deconstructionists, wannabe poets, militant lesbians, flamboyant fags, and a small collection of students on the seven-year plan. All of us socially awkward. All of us flaunting our uniqueness. All of us sharing a painful longing to fit in.

These round table discussions were our weekly haven. Every Friday we'd make the pilgrimage to the Blue Moon—the dirtiest bar with the cheapest drinks within walking distance of the college campus. We'd saunter in, grab the big, beer-stained table in the corner window and talk and drink and try to get lucky.

But I was only talking to one of them.

Her name was Fiona Franklin, and she had just been released from prison. Without any real malice or regret, she had shot her boyfriend in the face with a 12-gauge shotgun. She tells the story plain and simple. They were fighting. He was cranked up on smack. He handed her the gun and dared her to shoot. She did.

She was beautifully broken, and I wanted her.

Of course, she was a Women's Studies majoring comfortable shoes, and I knew I didn't stand a chance. I had unsuccessfully played out the same scenario at least a hundred times with the same number of women. That only encouraged me.

I leaned forward, speaking loud enough for everyone to hear, but secretly hoping with every word that some idea or phrase would spark a connection with the woman sitting next to me.

"The secret to time travel lies in molecular memory," I explained. "You see, every atom in existence has its own history. It has seen and done any number of incredible things since the beginning of time, and those experiences have been implanted in the unconscious 'consciousnesses' of these building blocks of the universe."

A few heads nodded, pretending to understand. The faces on the rest were blank.

Sarah, our heavily pierced angry poet, thought she got it, but she didn't. "So, what you're saying is that atom bombs are good because they release knowledge in the world?" she asked.

"Interesting thought, but no," I sighed, and tried again.

"Okay, everyone has heard of the collective consciousness," I explained. "Well, even though it sounds like a lot of psychological mumbo jumbo, it isn't. In fact, it's not spiritual or esoteric in any way. The collective consciousness is simply the knowledge of all time stored in the atoms and matter we see, touch, and smell every day, and every now and then people accidentally tap into it. You've heard of people having déjà vu or psychic visions? These people are unwittingly accessing the memories of the matter surrounding them."

I heard a guffaw. Myron, our resident suicidal psych major, was offended. "Please, don't bring Jung into your demented interpretation of the universe," he pleaded. "I'm pretty sure that whatever you're getting at is deeply offensive to the Jungian gestalt."

Another deep sigh. A swig of beer. I decided to speak very slowly.

"Did you ever wish you were a fly on the wall at some great historic event?" I asked. "Well, imagine the fly is the wall, and that wall is a recording device. Everything that has happened to that wall is constantly being recorded, and all we need to do is discover a way to play that recording back in a way that the human brain can understand it."

Third time's the charm.

Fiona nodded and her long black hair bounced provocatively on her shoulders. She got it. "I understand what you're saying, Jack," she said. "Imagine being able to know exactly what happened at Area 51 just by scooping up a handful of New Mexico sand and running it through a machine, or imagine the information you could get from a murder victim's clothes... But what does that have to do with time travel?"

Before I could answer, the peanut gallery chimed in.

John looked horrified. After two years in seminary, he had tossed out his bible to find salvation in Soren Kierkegard, Jean Paul Sartre, and other thinkers who were brave enough to use their real names. He was the group's self-proclaimed moral compass.

"Forget Area 51," he blurted. "A discovery like that would turn the world upside down. Do we really want to know the truth about Jesus Christ?"

"Or Kennedy's assassination?" Myron interjected.

"And what about the 'poor' husband who is so careful to shower off the perfume and remove the lipstick from his zipper only to come home to a wife with the ultimate lie detector?" Sarah laughed.

Fiona frowned, scrunching her forehead into delicate thought wrinkles. "Are we better off living in a world based on truth or is it to our advantage to have a chosen few fabricate reality for us," she said.

I agreed. "It really is just that simple," I said. "Science is like religion. We live in a binary world. At its root, there are only two options—truth or lies, good or bad. After that, the priests and the prophets complicate everything."

"The prophets of science?" John asked.

"People like you," I said and smiled. "People who try to make things more complex than they really are so they can sound smart and feel important."

The crowd chuckled. John looked to see if I was really insulting him. I was.

"Regardless of the implications, the science is incontrovertible," I continued. "The answers are there. We just have to find a way to get at them."

I paused for effect. The amateur think tank was listening with practiced skepticism.

"I have found that way."

Earlier in the semester, using a hefty investment from the Adult Entertainment industry interested in creating the first truly immersive virtual reality experience, I had developed the breakthrough technology that translated molecular memories into electro-chemical impulses that could be input directly into the human brain. Using an artifact or any object from a specific region or time period, my system would scan the individual atoms, "transport" my total awareness to that period of time, and allow me to interact with it.

It sounds easy, but it wasn't. That last bit was the tricky part. The first episodes of virtual time travel where limited to panoramic observations of history, but the experience only included general sights, sounds, and smells of the moment in time and space being replayed. Great for fact finding, but not very entertaining.

Now, don't get me wrong. That was pretty incredible, but I wanted more. So, I set out to generate the comprehensive artificial intelligence program that would allow me to interact directly with the electro-chemical impulses being poured into my brain. This new experience would include all of the senses, allowing me to touch the world in my head, speak with historical figures, and change history—at least in the virtual world. It was the best of all possible scenarios—you could travel in time without having to worry about destroying the space-time continuum or, even worse, becoming your own father.

To be perfectly honest, when I had finally hammered out the last algorithm and attached the last wire, I amazed even myself.

But the investors were not impressed. At the private unveiling of my masterpiece, they were irate. While they liked the idea that their customers could go back through time and chase down skirt from any era, they objected to the process.

"Look at all this crap," one pin-striped executive asserted, pointing to the cranial interface and the maze of wires and gadgets that made up the system. "Where does the penis go? Climbing into this thing is like climbing into an electric chair. I can't market this. It's not sexy at all."

He frowned at his colleagues, shaking his head. "Why would anyone buy this death trap when they can pick up a battery operated vagina at their local smut shop for $39.99?" he asked.

What could I do? They held the purse strings, so I streamlined the packaging to meet the unique needs of my clients. Three months later, the porn execs were thrilled. It was sleek and sexy, and they couldn't wait to get the Orgasmatron on the market.

Of course, when I shared my story at the Blue Moon, nobody believed me. They thought I was just another one of them. Lots of talk, a few published papers in obscure academic journals, and no action.

"Your Nobel Prize discovery raises a very interesting question," John said, mockingly. "If you could travel through time and have sex with any person alive or dead, who would it be?"

John was famous for his lists, and I was thankful. It gave me an opportunity to pour another beer, sit back, and evaluate the arena.

As usual, John answered his own question first. He was a pompous ass, and not very original. "Without a doubt, it would have to be Norma Jean," he said with a far off look in his eye. "Marilyn Monroe. Of course, it would have to be in her younger years before Einstein and Joe Dimaggio. I'm not into sloppy seconds."

The list that followed was equally unimaginative. The girls and one of the guys were hung up on Errol Flynn, Brad Pitt and Fabio. The guys mostly agreed with John, but added their own twists by limiting it to a specific movie character or hairstyle. I couldn't bring myself to admit that I'd already made the attempt many times. Turns out Marilyn was not as easy as I dreamed she'd be.

The discussion was getting tired, and I knew I was going to have to bring it back to life. Luckily, Fiona came to the rescue.

“I’d fuck Jesus Christ,” she said. “He’s certainly screwed all of us, and I wouldn’t mind returning the favor.”

Fiona had crossed a line. John’s jaw dropped, and his face went red. The table was stunned to silence. Despite the common belief that we were all rebel thinkers fighting to transform the world, the truth was most of us were just middle class white kids executing the comfortable legacy of our middle class heritage.

I jumped at the opportunity to defend her. “I understand what you mean. Who can resist a scraggly guy in sandals, and who knows what little tricks of the trade he picked up from Mary Magdalene? But for me, the son of God can take a number. If I could travel through time to sleep with anyone…”

I paused again, draining my beer for dramatic effect.

“I would travel five years into the future and have sex with myself.”

And that, my friends, was my moment of brilliance.

Fiona laughed. Actually, everyone was laughing, but the only one that mattered was the long-haired, murdering lesbian sitting next to me.

“No, I’m serious,” I explained, and I was serious. “Think of it. Who knows how to please me better than myself? Who knows my deepest fantasies and desires? Who else…”

I absent-mindedly put my hand on Fiona’s arm thinking there was a moment of connection between us. She immediately withdrew it and looked away uncomfortably.

The blatant rejection stung.

“Who else would be able to stand you with your clothes off,” John snorted. “Leave it to Jack to use the greatest scientific breakthrough of all time to come up with a new way to masturbate.”

Pissed on and insulted in less than a second, I let the barb go unanswered. My mind was now a whirlwind of numbers and theories. If my virtual time-travel machine could analyze molecular memory and extrapolate realistic outcomes from random factors inserted into the past, why couldn’t it draw on its vast and ever-growing knowledge of the human experience to accurately project settings and scenarios set in the future? Why couldn’t I travel five years into the future and have sex with myself?

Surely, that would be an adventure worth sharing at some

future Blue Moon round table discussion.

And I knew I was a sure thing.

I spent the next three days working around the clock. I fed as much of my life into the system as possible. Childhood photos (not that the pictures mattered, just the atoms they contained), important memorabilia, journals, clothes, anything I could find to build the database of me. At the same time, I fine-tuned the long strings of numbers and equations that made up the soul of my system's artificial intelligence.

Then I was ready.

I pulled back the stainless steel lid to the sensory deprivation tank that allowed my mind to experience sensations without the confusion of conflicting messages from my real body. I undressed, stepped in and carefully connected the condom electrode that allowed the system to communicate directly with my brain. Once the primary interface was firmly attached, I laid down, closed the lid and waited for the familiar nausea to wash over me.

First blackness. Then a frenetic race of jumbled pictures and sensations. It was like a DVD speeding forward to the good part of the movie. Then I was standing in front of a dark green apartment door in a posh apartment building or hotel. Taking a deep breath, beginning to feel a little excited, I knocked.

"Hello?" a voice called out. "Come on in. The door is open."

Thank God I had remembered to add clothing to the program.

I opened the door and stepped in. Nothing surprised me. It was a perfect mess, and I felt at home immediately. Light poured in from a wall of windows onto tables stacked with magazines, books and unrecognizable gadgets. An unmade bed was in the back left corner. The kitchen to the right was cluttered with empty beer bottles and Chinese take-out cartons. An oversized couch and armchair framed a humungous coffee table in the center. Everything in the giant studio looked half-read or half-completed.

A door on the opposite side of the room opened, and there I was.

I was coming out of the bathroom wet from the shower, wearing a luxuriously soft and clean bathrobe, leaving wet footprints on the plush white carpet. I looked at myself with just a little wonder. I was a tad older and a tad heavier, but I looked good.

I smiled. If this is my future, I thought, I'm okay with that.

However, the other me was not smiling. His forehead was creased with sudden hard thought, and his lips were twisted in reproach. Clearly, he recognized who I was, and he was not happy about it.

"What in the hell have I done?" he asked.

He surprised me. It wasn't quite the reception I was looking for, but I decided to roll with it. "That answers my first question," I said, walking into the room, picking up a magazine from the coffee table. No matter how hard I concentrated, the words would not come into focus. "I was wondering if you would be expecting me."

He looked me up and down, shaking his head. I saw realization wash across his face. Then, with a soft sigh, he went to the kitchen, pulled two beers out of the fridge and handed one to me.

"My guess is that you programmed the Orgasmatron with as much of your past as possible in order to generate my existence and visit me here today," he said. "Since you had not yet traveled to the future, none of the adventure you're currently experiencing was used to build this virtual world. All of this is original. It's happening to both of us for the first time."

Damn I was smart.

"There's a first time for everything," I added.

"That's the hope that keeps me going."

Without shame or hesitation, he threw his robe on the bed and pulled a familiar pair of flannel pajama pants off the back of the couch. He put them on just like me—one leg at a time, but he was very different. His eyes were on fire. I could feel the brilliance churning beneath the surface of the conversation. He was alive with a spark of creativity bursting to get out, and he moved with the confidence of a man who is used to transforming fantastic dreams into concrete reality.

I watched in awe as he paced the room.

I was glad the beer and liquor had not claimed too many of my brain cells—at least too many of the important ones. I downed half the bottle of imported ale, relishing the accuracy of the virtual taste. Virtual drinking was, in fact, one of my favorite aspects of time travel. I could drink an ocean of beer, get completely blotto, and then pop back to reality to skip the vomiting, hangover and calories.

I finished the bottle.

"So, you don't know why I'm here?" I asked.

"I imagine it's because your life is a mess and you're looking for guidance," he answered, handing me his unfinished beer. "Here, let me make it simple for you. Embrace the mess."

He paused, looking for my reaction. "Everything that's tormenting you now becomes the foundation for your success," he explained. "Right now, you feel like you don't fit in. No one understands you, and the people who pretend to understand make you want to punch them in the face. But take it from me, the depression, the angst, the desperation, they all lead to something much greater than you can possibly imagine."

I shook my head, wondering how to forward my agenda. He had no clue what was going on.

"Actually, that's not the reason at all," I said, taking a seat on the couch. "I'm here because I think there's a possibility that the two of us working together can take a plunge into completely uncharted territory. I was hoping you could help me out with a little experiment."

He stopped in his tracks and tilted his head. I could see the question in his eyes. Was I thinking something that he had never thought of before?

"Okay, I'm listening."

"Human relationships are like the fundamental macrobiotic biochemical principals that drive the Orgasmatron," I explained. "As you know, the Orgasmatron works best if the input consists of raw molecular matter from the exact time, place and person you want to create or recreate."

He nodded. "Yes," he said. "The closer the match, the easier it is for the system to generate the reality. That way the system doesn't have to sift through eons of irrelevant history or splice together recorded molecular memories from multiple items to create a cohesive target destination. Plain and simple, it's a lot less work."

I smiled. He understood. "I think the same thing could be said about people," I added. "The idea that opposites attract is baloney. The more different people are, the harder it is to synchronize their interface as human beings. With so little tying them together, they spend all of their time trying to fill the gaps between their realities."

"And, of course," he said, "most people fill those gaps with arguments or futile efforts to make the other person more like them. As a result, the compound binding the two people is based on negative energy, which ultimately leads to the devastating destruction of the bond or the relationship."

"Exactly," I said. I was getting excited. He was following my line of thought exactly. "On the other hand, the more alike two people are, the more organic and natural the bond between them is. This solid connection reinforced by the laws of nature is really the only possible foundation for a truly intimate and lasting joining of human souls."

The other me laughed out loud.

"Okay, wait, let me guess," he said, still chuckling under his breath. "You created me, this time, this place...you went to all this work so you could have sex with me. You think that you and I are organic matches. You think that because you and I are the same person and therefore so much alike, you'll finally find the intimacy you're looking for."

I looked him in the eye with hopeful anticipation. He shook his head.

"Now I need a beer," he said.

He walked to the kitchen, grabbed a bottle and drank it completely before sitting down on the couch next to me.

"I vaguely remember entertaining that thought about five years ago," he admitted. "I blurted it out at some bar to get a reaction out of some chick. I even remember working out the mathematics and temporal theories to support it. Fortunately, I was smart enough not to follow through with it."

He gave me a patronizing smile, lounged back on the couch and laughed again. "Sorry to disappoint you, brother," he said. "It just ain't gonna happen."

"But..."

"Oh, I know what you were thinking. You were tired of being alone. Tired of rejection. Tired of the shallow relief you give yourself on a regular basis. So, you thought of this new twist."

He gestured around the room and shrugged. "Let me ask you this, why did you travel into the future instead of the past to live out this Narcissistic fantasy?"

It was a good question, and I didn't know the answer. Traveling into the past would have been so much easier. The system was already in place. There was no need for any additional science or programming. Why did I go to so much trouble for this encounter with the future me?

Luckily, it was a rhetorical question. "I'll tell you why," he continued, holding my attention with his gaze. "When you think of yourself in the future, there's a natural appeal. You assumed I would be a better version of yourself. Smarter. More successful. More together. You want to explore the mystery of yourself. You want to know that person. You want to be that person."

I nodded. He was right.

"But the truth is that I'm sitting here in my virtual reality looking at me from five years ago. And to tell you the truth, I'm a little disgusted. Five years ago, I was self-absorbed, boorish, lonely, and so full of myself that nobody could stand to be around me. I was lost, and I didn't even know it."

He leaned forward and put his hand comfortingly on my knee. "I'm not that person any more," he said. "I'm not you, and to be perfectly honest, you are the last person in this world that I would ever want to sleep with."

Rejection. I felt my face burn and my head drop. I was speechless and ashamed, and I couldn't look him in the eye. How big a failure do you have to be to get turned down by yourself. Where do you turn when autoeroticism isn't an option?

"Oh, don't look so miserable," he consoled. "It's not so bad. The good news is right in front of you. You're wildly successful. The Orgasmatron is outlawed by the government, blackballed by academia, and officially denounced by the Catholic Church. The Pope himself called you a vile minion of Satan, so, of course, you make millions. You live an incredible life, driven by creativity, and your gadgets spearhead a revolution in scientific thought."

He held his hands out palm up like Jesus Christ at the last supper and gestured around the room.

"In time, my child, all of this will be yours," he mused.

His attempt at kindness and reassurance unknowingly pierced my heart, and raw despair flooded my chest. Looking around the room, I noticed there were no pictures, no postcards, no traces of any other human life. The first formula I ever invented came to mind.

"But I am still alone," I mumbled.

Without waiting for a response, I ended the program. Back in the real world, I slowly detached myself from the system with shaking hands, slid out of the lukewarm water, and sat naked and dripping on the cold laboratory floor. My heart sobbed. It might have been hours. It might have been days. I don't know. But when I rose, I rose with purpose.

$E = mc^2$

Where:

m = Your humility

c = Your compassion for the people around you

E = Your capacity for love

Einstein eat your heart out.

It was Friday night again, and I knew what I had to do. Hard to imagine all that had taken place in the last week, and yet everything was the same as always. The same faces sucking down the same drinks in the same corner of the same bar having the same conversations. It was beautiful, and I was scared.

As I entered the Blue Moon, John looked up from the incomprehensible illustration Myron was passionately scrawling on a napkin. "Hey, it's our very own Alexander Hartdegen, time traveler extraordinaire," he called out. "Is that primordial ooze on your pants or are you just happy to see us?"

I smiled, not knowing what to say, but determined to say something—despite my trembling voice.

"John," I said quietly. "You're an asshole, but I want you to know that I love you."

I sat down at the head of the table and refused the beer that was passed to me.

"In fact, I want all of you to know..." I spoke softly, looking down at my hands, "that I love each and every one of you."

I was searching for words, tripping over each thought as it came to me. Taking a deep breath, I looked around the table making connections one by one.

"This ad hoc gathering of iconoclastic outcasts...and freaks... is the highlight of my week," I continued, haltingly. "Every time I come here, I am totally blown away...by the ideas...and the passion…and the friendship you share…and I am deeply honored and humbled that you allow me to be a part of it."

The silence was thick and uncomfortable. They were waiting for the sarcastic punch line that would make everyone laugh.

"…and I know I don't deserve it."

Myron chuckled nervously. John looked away, embarrassed for me. The rest were still waiting.

Then I felt a hand on mine. I followed it up to Fiona's long black hair and a single tear in the corner of her eye. She smiled. When she spoke, there was a gentle invitation in her voice.

"So, having sex with yourself wasn't all it's cracked up to be?"

HONEY, IS THAT A DEAD HOOKER UNDER THE BED?

by J.A. Kazimer

"OH, YES," MRS. KRISTY MCMILLAN SAID, THRUSTING HER head against the fluffy, hotel pillow. The creak of the mattress springs kept a steady rhythm. The sexual symphony sounded vaguely like: *Creak…groan…oh, baby…harder…creak…* With an *oh, God, oh, yes,* thrown in for good measure.

Stan McMillan, the Waterbed King of the greater northeastern Peoria area and Kristy's husband of two and a half days, counted backwards from one thousand, trying to talk himself out of coming. The conversation in his brain went like this: *976...Don't do it...975…Cum now and she'll divorce you…974…Oh, God…SHIT!*

"Damn it." She smacked him in the head when he collapsed on top of her in an exhausted heap of spent, sweaty lust. Rolling his body off hers and onto the red satin sheets, she sat up. In the eerie glow of light streaming from the Las Vegas strip below, she opened the nightstand drawer, searching for her own satisfaction. Her hand brushed a leather bound bible, caressing the cheap inlayed gold.

Shit, where was it? Her hand pushed further back into the drawer, locating George, her vibrating companion, aptly named for the forty-third president. George was big, loud, and uncaring about poor Stan's premature incompetence issues.

She pulled George out and flicked him on. The low murmur of rattling plastic and batteries hummed throughout the room, as a pinpointed beam of light shot from the tip. George wasn't very bright, but it got the job done. More than she could say about her husband.

"Uuuuhhhhhaaa," she moaned, pressing the cold plastic to her.

"Honey?" Stan wrinkled his nose.

"What?!" Patience wasn't a virtue for Kristy, and neither was brains, but Stan loved her anyway. It might have had something to do with her d-cup breasts, thirty-inch waist, and bleach blonde hair. Big boobs, a mouth like a vacuum, and a hot body went a long way to make up for half-frozen dinners, and thousand dollar invoices from pet psychics. However, late at night, satiated and satisfied, Stan knew it went much deeper than the physical. They were two of a kind, two peas in the proverbial pod. His friends didn't understand what he saw in her, but they didn't know his terrible secret either. No one did.

He waved a hand in front of his nose. "Do you smell something?"

"If you are trying to get me to smell your farts, forget it." She turned George off, and switched on the light.

Stan frowned. "No…it smells like something died…"

Eyes narrowing, she sniffed the air. "Yewwww." She reached over him, picking up the hotel phone. Pressing zero, she waited for the operator to answer.

"How may I direct your call?" the polite voice on the phone asked.

"My room smells like death."

"Excuse me?"

Kristy repeated the comment. "My husband is paying twelve hundred a night for this suite, and it stinks." She could hear the clattering of keys on a keyboard.

Finally, the voice said, "Have you looked under the bed?"

"What?"

"Under the bed. This is Vegas after all." The voice sighed and hung up the phone.

She scrambled off the bed. "Move away from the bed!"

"What? What is it?" Stan glanced around, confusion and fear growing in his eyes.

She pointed to the mattress, and he shrugged his shoulders in question. She indicated again, stomping her foot. "Look under the mattress, you jerk."

Gripping the edge of the bed, he tugged. The mattress slid a few inches to the right. Kristy stood behind him, peering into the darkness. "I can't see anything. Can you?"

He shook his head.

"Pull it all the way off."

Swallowing hard, he did as she asked. The mattress fell onto his foot. "Fuck," he squealed and jumped around, arms flailing like a skittish cat. His fist smashed into the glitzy Tiffany lamp on the nightstand, knocking it to the floor with a crash. Bits of glass flew everywhere and the room went dark.

"Fuck," Kristy echoed, as he slammed into her, knocking her to the shag pink carpeting. Stan, naked and hopping on one foot, ran into the nightstand again, sending 'George' and himself flying backwards into the bed frame. There was a loud bang, and then dead silence.

"Stan?" she ventured from her place on the floor. "Honey, are you hurt?"

"Call an ambulance!"

"Oh, baby. Did you break something?" She stumbled to the phone, dialing 911.

A weak beam of light shot from inside the bed frame, as did the buzz of George on high speed. "Not exactly."

Kristy gazed into the bed frame. Stan lay sprawled on top of what looked like a dead body. In one of Stan's hands was George, and in the other, a prosthetic leg with bright purple toenails airbrushed onto its stubby plastic toes. Kristy's scream echoed along the strip twenty stories below.

◊◊◊◊◊

"Until two hours ago, you had no idea there was a dead hooker under the bed?" A bored cop in a bright yellow oxford shirt asked Kristy. They were standing in the hallway outside the suite, waiting for the crime scene technicians to clear it.

Nodding, she wiped her eyes with a snotty tissue. "How could this have happened?"

"Well, this is Vegas after all." He shrugged. "We get three or four of these cases a year. Fucking tourist." He paused. "No offense."

"How long had that poor…woman…been down there?"

The cop took out a notebook, and flipped through a few pages. "Looks like twenty-four to forty-eight hours. Your husband was a lucky man." She glared at him, and he quickly added, "If the body had been in full rigor when he landed on top of her, he might have been hurt."

Twisting her wedding ring, she declared, "But we've been in this suite for the last two and a half days."

The cop's eyes narrowed. "Have you been with Stan the entire time?"

Her face paled. "Stan would never do something like this. He wouldn't hurt a fly." Doubt crept into her eyes. "Of course, his first wife died under mysterious circumstances…"

"Tell me about it."

"Well, you see, I met Stan six months ago. He'd been widowed for four…"

The cop touched the tip of his pen to paper and took notes as Kristy told him all about Stan. At one point, his hand cramped and he had to ask her to slow down. Fifteen minutes later, the sordid tale of Stan's first wife's death, and how he couldn't satisfy Kristy in bed were duly noted.

◊◊◊◊◊

"Mr. McMillan, we have your fingerprints all over the victim, as well as DNA. A casino camera caught you in the bar chatting with her three hours before. Why don't you just tell me what happened?" A plain-clothes detective said in a friendly tone. His freshly pressed suit, and product-slicked hair made Stan feel like a bum in comparison. Stan's hair stuck up at odd angles, and he wore a pink hotel bathrobe.

"I told you already, Officer." Detective G.P. Roberts was neatly typed on the shiny metal of the detective's badge, but Stan refused to call him Detective. "My fingerprints and…other stuff…got on her body when I fell on top of her. As for talking to her in the bar, I have no idea what you are talking about. I'd never even met her." Stan shook his head.

That was the truth, wasn't it? He closed his eyes, and pictured her face—eyes and mouth wide—eyes vacant, so like his mother's. She looked like something out of a Wes Craven flick, a thick sheen of plastic reflecting off the dildo-flashlight. Like Freddy Krueger in a bad porno movie.

"She was a beautiful woman…well, if you could overlook the prosthetic leg and the penis…" Detective Roberts smiled, as Stan flinched. "Was that why you killed her? Because she was a man?"

"She was a man?"

"Yes, born Radcliff Reginald the Third."

Stan gave a whole body shiver. "He…she…looked like a woman…"

The detective shrugged. "This is Las Vegas—Drag Queen capital of the World." He leaned forward, resting his meaty arms against the table. "So the two of you got acquainted at the bar, you invited her up to your room for a little action while the misses took in a show, you got what you wanted—a little sucky, a little fucky—and blam out comes her penis and all bets are off. So you wrapped a Glad bag around her head…"

"No!" Stan threw his hands over his ears. "I didn't kill her… him." He pounded his fist on the table, the pink sleeves of the housecoat muting his ire. "I didn't kill anyone."

"Not even your first wife?"

Stan's mouth opened, but nothing came out.

"Mrs. Debra McMillan was found inside the trash can of the family home." The detective read from a file. "The cause of death was asphyxiation. The lead investigator believed she tripped and fell into the waste basket, which conveniently tangled around her head as she slowly suffocated to death."

Stan squeaked, "How…

"Now do you want to keep playing games or are you going to come clean?"

Stan sighed. This was going to be a long night.

◊ ◊ ◊ ◊ ◊

"Will the defendant please rise?" a tall, African American bailiff said, gesturing to Stan.

He shuffled to his feet. A grim-faced lawyer stood next to him, staring at the tabletop. Kristy, dressed in black as if she was attending a funeral rather than a trial, sat directly behind him, softly sniffling into a red, silk handkerchief. Stan swallowed hard, and faced the judge.

The honorable William Legacy read from a small slip of paper. "In the matter of the state of Nevada versus Stanley Homer McMillan, what say you?" he asked the juror foreman, a man with sharp, irregular features and an ulcer.

The foreman stood, clearing his throat like a cat with a

hairball. "We, the jury," he paused looking directly at Stan, "find the defendant guilty of second degree murder."

With a choked cry, Kristy jumped from her seat. "Nooooo," she wailed, grasping at an emotionless Stan as he was dragged away in handcuffs. Detective G. P. Roberts nodded in satisfaction—one more dirt bag off the streets.

◊◊◊◊◊

Later that night, after giving interviews to all the local news stations, Kristy sat, sipping a vodka martini and flipping through the hundreds of hotel porno stations. Her thoughts drifted to Stan. He had looked devastated as the cops led him off—almost defeated—a broken shell of the once powerful Waterbed King. She rubbed her tired eyes, and shakily stood. Too much vodka, she thought, weaving slightly.

Heading into the bathroom, she stripped off her black dress. Underneath she wore nothing but lotion and sheer onyx stockings. She twisted the shower knob to hot, and stepped into the steamy water, letting it run along her cellulite-free body.

Bang.

Kristy jumped, her heart slamming wildly in her overdeveloped chest. She quickly shut off the water, and grabbed a towel. "Hello?" she tentatively called. "Is anyone there?"

No response.

She made her way into the bedroom, carefully searching the shadows. Nothing. Sighing with relief, she sat on the waterbed, running her fingers through her wet hair. Drips of water formed a puddle on the carpeting underneath her feet.

A voice from the shadows of the thick fabric curtains whispered, "Did you look under the bed?"

Kristy screamed, dropping her towel.

The curtain moved and from the darkness, Detective G. P. Roberts stepped out.

"Where the hell have you been?" Kristy asked, throwing herself into his arms. "I've been waiting for over an hour."

"Can't get enough of me?"

She smiled—a demure, coy smile meant to tempt, tease, and ultimately bring a man to his knees. "More like I want to make sure you don't fuck this up. Jail is no place for a lady."

He looked hurt. "When have I ever made a mistake?"

She tilted her head. "That's true."

Carrying her to the bed, he dropped her onto the red satin sheets. The water filled bed sloshed and her silicone breasts rode the wave like a pro. He came down next to her, sliding his hands along her shapely curves with a smirk. "It makes me nuts to think of his hands on you."

Pulling at G.P.'s belt, she smiled. "They weren't on me all that long. As a matter of fact, I had a more fulfilling relationship with a tube of plastic."

"Well, I'm here to make you forget all about your plastic pal, George…"

As if he could, she thought with a grin.

◊◊◊◊◊

Two hours later, G.P. had been good to his word. Kristy yawned and stretched like a well-fed black widow, smiling lazily at his muscled body. "Where ever did you find a transvestite, one-legged hooker?"

He shrugged. "A dumpster next to Circus Circus. He'd been dead a day or so."

"I almost shit when I saw the leg. You could have warned me." She playfully tugged on his dark chest hair.

He laughed. "I wanted it to be a surprise."

"That it was." She sat up, pulling the sheet over her breasts. "The videotape in the bar…how did you do that?"

"I hired some hooker to approach dear old Stan, make it look like he was looking for some action." He twisted a blonde lock of her hair through his fingers. "The video was grainy, and the bar is pretty dark. It could have been anyone. But as long as the jury bought it, that's all that mattered."

"Good point. And buy it they did." She laughed, thinking of the jurors' disgusted faces as they watched Stan pick up a gimpy transvestite.

"So Mrs. McMillan, what do you plan to do with your jailbird husband's millions?"

Closing her eyes, she pictured all the things she would do, and buy—a houseboat on the Rivera, a ski cabin in Vail, and a winery in Napa…

"Why didn't you just kill him outright?" G.P. asked, scratching his head.

For a detective, he wasn't all that bright. "If he died, half of the estate would go to his various relatives and friends. Hell, even his maid gets a couple thousand." She shook her head. "No, I want it all. I deserve it too after putting up with his slobbery kisses, sweaty balls, and premature ejaculation."

"You are one cold hearted woman," G.P. said, kissing her neck. "You always have been."

"And that's what you love about me." She kissed him, trapping his hands against the headboard with thick, silk scarves. He smiled, closing his eyes as she wound the bonds around his wrists. Let the games begin…

◊ ◊ ◊ ◊ ◊

In the mirror above the bed, Kristy watched G.P. sleep, his hands still tied to the bed. How innocent and sweet he looked, like a child resting after a long, hard day at play. She smiled, and kissed his forehead. He moaned, but didn't return to consciousness.

Her hand moved toward the nightstand, a smile on her face. She let her fingers do the walking, shifting from side to side until they found the ultimate prize. Ah, she thought, as they touched the cold, shimmering plastic. Quietly, she pulled it out, excitement filling her.

"What th—," was all G.P. could get out before the plastic bag was wrapped tightly around his face. He struggled against his bonds, weakening as oxygen slowly seeped from his blood. His lungs burned, and his brain began to shut down. The last thing he saw through the clear plastic was Kristy's smiling face and the love of her life, a ten-inch vibrator named, George.

SPOCK: A ROMANCE IN QUOTES

by Kristen McHenry

We met by chance on a Sunday
at the town aquarium.
He stood aloof in the octopus exhibit,
gazing at their writhing tentacles, and looking
inscrutably pained. He turned to me and said,
"They regard themselves as aliens
in their own world, a condition
with which I am somewhat familiar."
I fell in love right there.

He came over to drink vodka
Gimlets on my porch swing,
and read to me from "Entropy".
At first he was a bit standoffish,
but when we finally did make love,
he whispered, "Random chance
seems to have operated in our favor."

He moved in on Tuesday.

When we fought,
he would squint at me with his satanic eyes
then say something unarguably rational,
without rancor, without
smashing plates. That was the thing about Spock:
he could be always be trusted
not to smash things, not to shove his fists
through the drywall in a rage, or fly
into a temper on the freeway.
He just dealt with things. For a while, it was bliss.

Then his unflappable
demeanor began to try my nerves,
at which time he observed, "It is curious
how often you humans manage to obtain
that which you do not want."

On Friday, he said he was leaving,
not just me, but the planet. "Nowhere
am I more desperately needed
as among a shipload of illogical humans."

When I threw myself onto the futon and sobbed,
he stroked my hand and said, "You may find that
 having
is not so pleasing a thing as wanting. This is not
logical, but it is often true."

When I bellowed that he was a cold-hearted
bastard, he looked away. "I am what I am,
and if there are self-made
purgatories, then we all have to live in them. Mine
can be no worse than someone else's."

And when I shattered all the plates and screamed
that he was throwing away a beautiful thing,
he just shrugged. "It has always been easier
to destroy than to create."

Then he packed his belt and tunic, and walked out.

Spock's been gone awhile now.
I still wear his Command badge on my bathrobe.
At night, I fumble for it, and hear
his sonorous voice: "Logic is the beginning
of wisdom; not the end."

ON THE MANY USES OF DUCT TAPE FOR RESOLVING RELATIONSIHP ISSUES

by Terrie Leigh Relf

You're right!
We DO need to end this…
But first,
give me a hand
with this package…

What's in the box?
A few nick-knacks
to put in storage:
a little of this,
yes—that, too…
but mostly
what's left of you.

When Molly the Necrophiliac Went on a Date With Suicide Stanley

by Match Ryan

MOLLY PUSHED HER INDEX FINGER AGAINST THE tip of her nose, as if it were a button that could heighten the smell of pre-death. "I love this aroma of anticipation," she said to Stanley, who was marinating in a tub of cold water.

Stanley held his elbows and shivered. When he spoke, his teeth clacked together. "I thought we were gonna have sex."

"Way too early for that." She opened her mouth and winked, as if he just might like what she had planned.

Molly had initially found out about Stanley when visiting her therapist friend. Upon snooping through some confidential files, she'd found the following note scribbled at the bottom of a page: Stanley is the most suicidal client I've ever had.

Molly had shared many of her quirky ideas with her therapist friend, including her philosophy on prescription birth control: It wasn't foolproof; therefore, she wouldn't use it. If you climbed into bed with a warm body, no matter what precautions you took, you could get pregnant.

Molly didn't like babies. She found it annoying that they had so much life ahead of them. She preferred dead people, who had their whole life behind them.

"Here you go." Molly pressed down on the top of a red click pen. Excitement shot through every vein in her body, and she could feel her blood lighten and percolate, as if a champagne cork had been pulled and the celebration was about to begin. She placed the pen in Stanley's right hand—the hand she'd made him keep dry.

Stanley nodded and began to cry. His tears made her think of embalming chemicals leaking from a corpse; the foamy soap around his nipples reminded her of a lactating mother more than a lover that she was about to experience; his fingernails were long enough to pick a banjo.

"Remember, vertical not horizontal." Upon her leaving the room, Molly pointed at a white pad of paper.

Her strategy for remaining barren stayed a secret, but her proclivity for dating suicidal men became a constant source of gossip and speculation. Afraid of picking up a charge of assisting suicide, she moved on to other types of men: chemo patients, death row inhabitants, and when desperate, she trolled the interstate for fresh traffic accidents.

Eventually, her pregnancy fears began to increase. What if there were a small amount of postmortem emission? Did such a thing exist? If sperm can live for 72 hours in open air, could it live for 72 hours inside a dead body?

Enough is enough, she decided. Molly started taking the pill, became a hospice nurse and only assisted men who, at same point in their life, had undergone a vasectomy.

It Might As Well Be Me

by Helen Silverstein

"HONEY, EMPTY THE DISHWASHER BEFORE YOU leave," Heather said to her husband, Gerald, as she was busily nursing their twins.

"Sure thing, sweetie pie. Love of my life," he answered, tickling the tops of her breasts. His two sons, tucked like footballs, one under each of her arms, sucked noisily on her nipples. It was a sweet spot, he recalled fondly, bending low to kiss each boy on the head. "My little guzzlers," he said, winking at his wife and blowing her a kiss as he turned on his heel. "I'd like to knock their noggins aside and get in there for a swig myself," he called to her, leaving quickly through the kitchen door, dishwasher left unemptied. How could a man remember a thing like that when he had just been witness to two others of his gender gorging on his wife's breasts? "Impossible!" He shouted happily.

Inside his briefcase he had THE BOOK that had changed his life. He headed straight for the coffee shop near where he worked. Slim chance his wife would emerge from the condo, given the hungry young twins she had in her care. But why chance it? Why ruin a perfectly good, why a beautiful day—heavenly—with even a whisper of doubt that he would be found out? No, better he should trot a bit farther and remove himself from the danger zone entirely.

Gerald had taken three personal days, on the advice of his therapist—so no guilt here, no sireee, just pure freedom and joy. Time for himself. The father, the provider, the one on whom all fiscal responsibility lay. The one who had been robbed of his wife's ample bosoms by the tiny twins—but he was not resentful. No! Quite to the contrary. He was doing what he needed to do to feed himself. To provide that all-important sense of freedom and zest for life. All around him he noticed exhausted, downtrodden, sleep-deprived, sex-deprived, wife-deprived fathers, falling into the trough of despair. But not Gerald. Oh no, not him. He would not fall into that trap. He patted his very light briefcase. Not with this inside.

Swinging into the coffee shop, finding his favorite window view corner table available, he thought, yes! This is a great day. He sat down with his double-shot mocha, extra whip and pulled out The Book: *If Only One of You Can Survive, It May as Well Be You.* "Thank you, thank you," he said thinking of his shrink, the author and purveyor of this incredible book. What a lifesaver, he thought, opening to chapter two, which was—wonder of wonders—entitled "Lifesaver," replete a colorful picture of that old time treat: a book of Lifesavers. What every kid wanted as part of his (hopefully) plentiful stack of stocking stuffers at Christmas.

Gerald placed a neat check mark next to the picture an orange lifesaver, the first in a colorful column of lifesaving tips.

"Make wise use of good natured forgetting when it comes to chores." No need to rush on to the next tip. No need to rush at all. Gerald intended to savor the orange lifesaver, his mouth puckering to suck, suck, suck.

Sharks With Thumbs

by DAVID JAMES KEATON

"What dost thou strike at, Marcus, with thy knife?"
"At that that I have killed, my lord, a fly."
"Out on thee, murderer! Thou killst my heart."
— William Shakespeare, *Titus Andronicus*

YOU EVER GET THE FEELING SOMEONE IS TALKING about you?

I'm right at the end of the movie when the speaker starts popping and I hear these words. Once a week, right when I'm finally starting to relax around this spiderweb of power cords and surge protectors, I'm reminded I can never trust the wiring around here. Never move somewhere just because you like seeing a river out your window.

I remember when a nearby lightning strike fried something inside the picture tube and put a freaky green line through the middle of the screen. That green line was there for about six months, mercifully getting smaller and smaller and almost fading away until it was just a glowing yellow smear in the corner of the TV, like I'd smashed a lightning bug on the glass and never cleaned it up. I don't know if this room is some sort of electric Bermuda Triangle, but I can't risk any more equipment and that's why I move fast whenever I hear a speaker snap, crackle, or pop.

I'm ready to pull the plug when suddenly I'm hearing two voices from the speaker that aren't part of the movie. I know this because the movie was at the end, right at the part where everyone gets what they deserve, and all I should be hearing is gunfire, one-liners and big, dumb music. However, this whispered conversation is something you'd hear in the middle of a flick, maybe the beginning, when you're not sure what the characters are really up to and you're supposed to be all suspicious of everyone.

The sad thing is he has no idea I hate his guts.

I sit down by the speaker, actually thinking about getting a glass to put between the television and my ear to hear the voices better.

Remember his last story? Even the goddamn dog was rolling his eyes.

I adjust my legs to get comfortable, hoping the reception lasts a while. I know "hearing voices" is supposed to make you nervous, but it happens in this building sometimes. A couple times, a year back, when my surround-sound speakers were still working, I picked up some random banter between truckers. It's the bad wiring that does it. Sometimes, you'll suddenly get three more people in the middle of your phone call, and you'll find yourself answering a question about the first time you stuck a finger up someone's ass instead of answering your grandpa's question about car insurance.

But those fractured conversations lasted a minute at the most, and they were nowhere near as clear as this. This is like I'm holding the tomato cans between two people, but their string's coming out both my ears.

If that bastard had any idea what people say…

Right then, the speaker crackles and the voices are buried under static. I lean in closer and bang my head on the glass. There's a final POP! and I yank the cord from the wall. I sit with my back to the TV, feeling the electricity tickle my neck as both me and the equipment power down. I reel in the cord, wrapping it around my knuckles, working to bend the prongs straight.

I hold my breath when I plug it back in. Thank Christ it still works. I stare at the green stain in the corner of the picture. It's back, but it doesn't bother me. I'd watch TV if the whole screen was green. Nothing happens in the corners of a movie anyway. A green sunset in this western? The gunfighters won't even notice.

00:00:03:57 - love without a life jacket

When I say there's a long list of things about her that used to drive me nuts, I'm not talking about a sheet of paper, or even a stack of paper with both sides filled plus illustrations in the margin and a flip-cartoon in the corner to re-enact the top ten, I'm talking about the kind of list where you could stand at the top of the stairs and you let the pages drop and they bounce down the steps and unroll out the door and down the hill and across the street and over the cars and stray dogs are crashing through it like a finish line. That's how long my list is. And at the top of that list? That would have to be the way she used to walk into the bathroom to use the phone. It drove me crazy. Well, crazy enough to ruin my day. Luckily, that's one thing I don't have to worry about anymore. This new girl I got? She stares right at me when she's on the phone. She let's me listen to the even her most embarrassing conversations. She's never turning the volume down on the receiver in case the caller says something I shouldn't hear. She's never pressing the phone hard against her head, so afraid a secret would sneak out while she was talking. So hard her ear looks like a ripe tomato slice when she finally snaps the phone shut.

This new girl? She's got nothing to hide. She's in the bathroom right now, and I trust her so much I'm not even turning down the volume to listen to her piss.

Then the toilet flushes once, twice, and chokes on a third attempt. She walks back into the room, then slides down to her hip in a quick motion that would make any gunfighter shake in his boots. My smile slips when I see her phone drop into her pocket.

"I thought you drowned," I tell her.

00:00:28:09 - bugs can't use tools

It's too cold to have a fly on the window, on either side of the glass. There's no leaves on trees. The birds are long gone. The morning before, I had to dig my car out from under the wake of a snowplow with red fingers. There's nothing alive outside without fur, nothing alive out there smaller than a rat. But there it is.

One of those big, blue-eyed garbage flies, crawling around

the edges of the glass like it was summer out there, like there isn't a kid kicking the head off a snowman two houses down. In a daze, I pull the black tape off the window, taking some of the paint with it, knowing it's going to take another hour to seal that window back up. I yank it up with a grunt, cold air freezing the snot in my nose. It's the first time I've ever seen a fly trying to get in instead of out.

What the hell do you feed it? Usually, you're trying to stop a fly from drinking off the edge of your pop can instead of keeping it alive. So I just stand back and let it ricochet off the walls like a drunk hoping it'll find a stray cornflake or damp toenail to munch on. I watch it circle the room about six more times, increasingly confused by its behavior, cruising frantic figure-eights about a foot from the ceiling. Finally, I grab a stuffed animal still upside down in a corner from three ex-girlfriend's ago and chase it toward the bathroom. If I'm going to have a pet fly it should be near the bowl, right? I mean, I'm a pretty clean dude, but I figure if there's anything around this place a fly can eat, it's going to be in there. Hell, cats and dogs get water bowls, don't they? I should write the name "Spike" on the side of my toilet.

00:00:42:31 - am I gonna eat what exactly?

The next day, this new girl comes over to watch a movie. Halfway through, the speakers start popping again, and while I'm screwing with the wires in the back of the box, she sighs and runs to the bathroom. And suddenly, I'm listening to her piss even though she's 100 feet and a closed door away. It's splashing so loud I flinch and think she squatted down over my head.

That's when I remember the fly.

Same old shit, you know? Why do I come over here?

The voice is fading, so I crawl over to my bookbag and pull out my headphones. I quickly try plugging the headphones directly into the TV and I get zapped with static instead. Like a fool I sit there, with the headphones unplugged and dangling, still listening for the voices. The headphones are new. They're the kind that go into your ears instead of over them, sometimes too deep, the kind that you might lose in your head if you scratch too hard. Like I do. And just like they always told me would happen when people are talking shit, my ears start burning.

I have to go watch the rest of this horrible movie, if he ever gets it to work...

I'm so excited about hearing someone's voice through unplugged headphones that, at first, I don't care what she's saying. It's not like the truckers I heard before. This time I can only hear one side of the conversation. Her voice is a non-stop sigh, like the endless hiss of a tire valve.

Maybe I'll pretend I'm sick.

Then the toilet flushes, and it's as loud as a hurricane. I grab the sides of the TV in case I start spinning around a drain and get sucked down. I'm so wired about this discovery that I'm smiling like a maniac when she comes out, struggling to keep my new eavesdropping skills to myself. By the time we finish the western, I realize it's not just the headphones. The fly was in there with her.

...the first time I've ever seen a fly trying to get in instead of out...

This new power is coming from the fly.

00:01:34:07 - spiders are not our friends

After she's gone home, I'm thinking I should call NASA or whatever government office deals with the physical manifestation of metaphors. Or, at the very least, spy on about ten more people I suspect are talking shit about me. I'm already making a mental list when I go back into the bathroom.

The fly is dying. At least, it's moving slower. My eyes follow its sluggish path until it vanishes into a crack in the porcelain box behind the toilet. I panic and shove the clock radio and empty box of tissues onto the floor and take off the lid, shaking my head in disbelief as I look inside. Impossible.

The fly is caught in a spiderweb, flailing like a drunk trying to navigate a beaded curtains at a party. Spiders in the toilets? Flies in the snow? What's next?

Suddenly, I know what to do. I tie it outside the bathroom window, and, just as I hoped, the cold air seems to revive it. It's moving fast again, but it never gets back to full speed. It's not going to last much longer. I check the clock radio on the bathroom floor to try and estimate how much time the fly has left. The display is flashing a green "12:00 a.m." since I never figured out how to set it. Now, I've got two problems. A time limit, I'm not good with math, and I can't get everyone into my bathroom to spy on them.

Staring at the word "Spike" on the bowl, I decide I should take my fly for a walk.

Once, my grandpa told me he used to stick flies to his fingers with honey when he was a boy.

"We were bored as hell back then," he said, "Now, don't think I'm reminiscing so I can tell you how it built character or any noble shit like that 'cause the only thing playing with flies does is make you wish you had toys instead."

He told me his flies didn't fly too long because he always smacked them just a little bit too hard to slow them down, sort of like my grandma.

Well, mine won't last long either. I have to move faster than I am.

I look around the bathroom, find some dental floss the last girl left behind.

I have no trouble grabbing it out of the air, and it's still sluggish enough to tie a leash around its body without risking a swat to stun it, but the floss is too thick for a knot. I look around and around and around, and finally my eyes stop on the answer stuck to the side of my toilet, underlining my pet fly's name. I crouch down to get closer.

All this time I thought it was a crack in the porcelain but it's a long black hair stuck to the moisture on the side of the bowl. I peel it loose and hold it up to the window. Black. One of hers. I half-expect it to twitch like a severed spider's leg. And even though it's just a hair, even though I haven't cleaned the bathroom since she left, I'm still amazed to find a piece of her still here. I'd be less surprised to find a five-foot-five layer of skin she'd shed, rustling and drying in a corner.

I tie the leash quick. Too easily. I decide it's because I had one of my hands buried in her hair for so many years that, when they're not connected to her head anymore, they still know my fingers and sometimes I can still get them to do what I want.

The fly grabs her hair and starts stroking it with two front legs. Does that damn thing have thumbs? Impossible. If bugs had tiny thumbs, they would have already invented the tiny wheel.

I tie it to my finger where the skin is still white from the ring she gave me. Then I put on headphones plugged into nothing, a power cord dangling down and tucked into a belt-loop. I start my day.

00:01:09:13 - bringing a fly to a fist fight

I'm out the door looking at my watch, and I see it's time for free doughnuts. The gas station makes new ones and throws out the old ones at exactly 8:00 every day. They're always real cool about giving me those old ones, but you got to time it just right. The fly tugs on its leash, circling my ring finger, then resigning to wrap itself around the steering wheel. I worry about a sudden turn breaking the leash, so I pull over and carefully unwind the hair without breaking it, thinking about the old westerns my grandpa used to make us watch, and the way the cowboys made their horse stay put by dropping a leather strap across a bush or twig without even tying it up or anything.

Inside the gas station, the girl behind the counter smiles, and I grab one of each kind of doughnut before the kid can slide them into the trash. He sighs and waits for me to drop them into my bag, then he quickly clears the case. I take longer than usual because I'm trying to keep one hand behind my back. I don't know what would be worse, someone thinking that flies follow me around, or someone seeing that I keep one a tiny little leash.

When she's counting the cigarettes behind her, I tie the fly to a bag of peanuts near the cash register, not really tying a knot, just winding the hair around the peanuts one time, then I run out to pump my gas.

Inside, I see the girl at the counter talking to the next guy in line and he throws a thumb my way. I quickly pull the headphones from inside my shirt and pop them in to see if this guy is talking shit. Amazingly , he isn't. But she is.

He just tries to act like he had no idea they were free even though he was in here last night…

My head down, I run in and grab my fly. For the first time since I started going there, she talks to me.

"You paying for those peanuts, asshole?"

I stop at the post office and check the stamp machines in the lobby. Just as I hoped, there's a wagging tongue of five three-cent stamps sticking out. I tear them free and put them in my pocket. Ever since the price of stamps went up, people usually leave the difference behind.

The girl behind the counter smiles and waves as I leave.

He doesn't have three cents?

What the hell? I scratch my ears hard to see if the voice goes away. If I could scratch my ears with my foot, I would. I don't understand. The headphones are around my wrist. The fly isn't anywhere near her. And neither am I.

I go to the diner. Are there girls behind every counter? Do they grow them back there, just out of sight? Are there ten more girls behind the counters you can't see yet only because they haven't grown high enough for their heads to clear the register?

A girl with the pencil shaped like a tiny pool cue. I stare at it, hypnotized, every time she takes my order. I asked her about it once, but she ignored me. Tonight is no different.

"Waitress, there is a fly in my soup…"

She looks down at the fly tugging against its leash on my finger. "…and I think the little bastard just lassoed me."

She wanders away, a miraculous combination of expressions on her face that I didn't think were possible.

I stop in the restroom on the way out. In the urinal, just above the line-of-fire, there's a sticker that declares: "You hold in your hand the power to stop a rape!"

For a second I think the sign refers to the fly crawling across my knuckles, and I'm suddenly ashamed. Is it so wrong to be "the fly whisperer?" When I'm zipping up, one headphone falls from my left ear and plops into the urinal. I sigh, pull the rest of the wires out of my shirt and toss them all in.

I stop at the garage to get air for my tires. It's the only place in town where you don't have to pay fifty cents to do this. The guy who owns the garage gives me a knowing smile and a wave. I wave back and accidentally bounce my fly off my forehead. He's cool. Last time I was there he agreed with me that paying for air is "freaking ridiculous."

I get out, tie the fly to the compressor, snake the hose, hit the button.

How fucking low do you have to be to steal air…c'mon.

Was that a girl's voice? I thought it was all guys in that garage. A girl from one of my earlier stops? What kind of reception does this fly get, anyway?

I heard of someone stealing dirt once, only that was from a construction site and that shit ain't cheap. But air? Nope. Never heard of anyone stealing air.

The compressor stops rumbling. My fly strains on its leash, then curls back to land on a coil of hose.

I've heard of people stealing water once, but that was during the war.

I throw the hose. 29 pounds will have to do.

Honestly, who the hell steals air…

I can't contain my rage any longer. I yell at the shadows in the garage.

"Who the hell sells air?!"

Two mechanics slides out from under a cars and into the sunlight. They stand up and walk toward me, wiping grease from their fists, blowing sweat off their noses, staring at me like I'm nuts.

00:01:45:22 - fly factory revealed

Do you ever get the feeling someone is talking shit about you?

I stop at the video store to steal some DVD inserts. I do this because they really are good reading. Sure, sometimes you get a paragraph of summary or some decent production notes or an interview, but that's not what I'm looking for. I steal the inserts because I like to read the chapter titles. It's like a whole movie in ten seconds. The chapter titles tell you all you need to know.

I grab a random one to prove my point. Okay, not so random:

Sharks With Guns

1. Love on a lifeboat
2. Sharks can't use tools
3. Are you gonna eat that?
4. Dolphins are not our friends!
5. Bringing a shark to a gun fight
6. Shark factory revealed!
7. Duel to the deaf
8. Quitting the Coast Guard

See? What are you missing from the story after you read that? It's all there. The crisis, the love interest, the surprise ending. Didn't someone once say there are really only three stories you can tell? A stranger comes to town, and a man goes on a journey? Man sort of talks to fly?

I study the box to the movie and snicker, as there's no way that shark could hold that chainsaw, much less a gun. They don't have any thumbs.

Now, that would be a scary movie. If they had thumbs, they could make a phone call. It wouldn't have to bite anyone. Just show one shark whip out a phone and every asshole in the audience would start screaming their head off.

Could happen. I've seen more far-fetched things than that in a movie. One time, in the bathtub, my ex-girlfriend checked her phone underwater so I couldn't see who called her. I figured she'd ruined it, but it turned out the phone worked fine when I blew the bubbles off of it later that night to check that number she was hiding.

I slip some DVD booklets into my sleeves then go up to the counter and grab one of those free internet CDs. She is up there, and I see a strange light flickering in her eyes, and I realize the girl is watching something under the register with the volume turned down. When did she sneak a TV in here?

Suddenly I have to know what movie she's watching. Is she watching something she's not supposed to? Why else would she have the volume down like that?

On the way out, I finally see what it is. A security monitor. She was watching me steal those inserts the entire time. I can see myself in the corner of her screen, standing by the door, hunched and alone, looking over her shoulder, guilty as hell, green as the sunset.

Sitting in the car with my hands on the steering wheel my heart jumps. The fly is dangling on the hair like a suicide. I turn on the air-conditioning, open all the vents, and hold it in front of the cold air. It starts to climb back up its leash like a spider. It's moving slow, but it's still alive. I realize that every time I hide the fly, it starts to die.

Sounds like a children's rhyme, doesn't it?

I have to get home. Or get it to the bathroom. Or a restroom. You ever notice how cold the water in a toilet is? Even on the hottest day? Even if you know what's been in there, it's got to be tempting to swim in it. For a bug, I mean.

I drive fast, checking the size of the gas stations, trying to gauge whether they're big enough for a public toilet. I glance down at the fly and see it slump on the string and swing from the hair like a pendulum. I slam on the brakes and make a hard right into the smallest gas station I've ever seen.

I ask the third-grader behind the counter if they have a restroom. He says no and turns back to counting the candy bars. In desperation, I hold up my hand with the limp fly swinging from my finger.

"Dude, my fly needs to drink from a toilet fast or it's going to die."

The kid smiles over a huge piece of gum and stares at me for 13…14…15 seconds. Then he points to the door behind the beer.

"Hurry up."

Unfuckingbelievable. Guess he's seen stranger things than this.

Inside the bathroom, I'm assaulted by a stench worse than any outhouse. I walk over to the toilet and cautiously lift the lid. The water is clear as a mountain spring. I carefully lower my hand until the fly's head just breaks the surface. I think about the part of the buddy-cop movie right around the second act where the drunk partner has to get revived by the wise-cracking partner, who shoves his face in the toilet. I'm much more gentle than that.

And it works. The fly starts to activate, cranking its legs over its head to clean itself off. I smile. It looks like it's playing a tiny air guitar. No, it would need thumbs to do that.

Back in the car, I wonder how many people would believe I'm actually worried about this fly. I try to imagine myself in the waiting room at the veterinarian. I'd be the only person that a kid with a sick hermit crab could feel good laughing at. I watch it perched on the radio knob, cleaning its wings.

I've spent more time worrying about this fly than I worried about my ex-girlfriend. Even when she had to get her appendix out. I mess with my stereo.

Equalizer. That's a good word.

Suddenly I understand something. It just seems like I care about the fly more than her, but if you were to line them up against the wall and put a little pencil mark over their heads, you'd find that actually my feelings about the fly and her are exactly the same. And it's not that I think more of a fly. It's just that, the more I find out about human beings, and the more I listen to their voices when they don't think anyone can hear, the less I think of them.

00:01:58:19 - ears are burning

One time I told her I was going to invent a phone that, instead of ringing, released a swarm of bees instead. I said it would guarantee she would answer the thing every time I needed her to. She didn't understand what the hell I was talking about. I think she thought I was talking about some special ringtone. I said, "okay, listen, how about just three small bees, just enough of a scare to buzz around your ears and make you swat the air in a panic every single time I called you?" She had no answer to that.

I walk out of the bathroom, and I see she was reading that same magazine again, the one with the prescription label with my ex-girlfriend's name on it. I even told her how she used to snort painkillers off those very same pages. You'd think that alone would make her not want to read it. I used to try to get a letter published in one of her magazines so she'd stumble across my name.

Wait, did I say "prescription" earlier? Because that is exactly what I meant.

The speaker suddenly starts popping again.

Shit fuck shit. I pull the cords on everything. I hate the wiring in this house. It eventually destroys everything. I hear water running in the sink, and I figure she's going to be in there awhile. She does that sometimes. Runs the sink so I can't hear. Like I'm really listening to hear her pissing. Suddenly I remember something, and I quickly crawl to my box of old cassette tapes rotting in the corner. It's my worst, last pair of headphones. Huge ratty ones from the '80s that cover your entire friggin' head. I hesitate to put them on.

My headphones are getting bigger and bigger as I seem to be sliding further back down the headphone-evolutionary ladder. Once I'm holding them in my hands and blowing the dust and insect shells off the foam, I realize they're older than I thought.

They're from the '70s, not the '80s, and they're the only thing left of my mom. One time, she came up to me and put these over my ears, and I was pouting about something, so I didn't say anything, didn't even look up, but I didn't take them off my ears either. And I still can't remember the song she wanted me to hear or why she wanted me to hear it. Maybe there was something funny in the song? Maybe the lyrics meant something to her? Maybe she thought it was my favorite band? I can't remember. I was too busy ignoring her. And now, I'll never know what it was because I just sat there, arms crossed, mad about something stupid I can't remember, frowning until the song was over and she finally walked away.

The wind blows the dead fly around on its string. My ring finger is white from lack of circulation. I unwrap the leash from my skin, waiting for the blood flow to return and paint the white knuckle red again. I'm amazed at how strong her hair was.

The strange thing is, when I think back to it, I could have sworn I was outside, sitting with crossed legs and crossed arms under a tree when she walked up and put these over my ears. The cord couldn't have reached that far, could it?

It's true that the bathroom is the last place where the remains of a relationship will linger. Is it all those half-empty bottles and soaps. Or is it just hairs around the toilet?

00:02:00:07 - end credits and ironic theme music

The next day I finally take out the trash. Not a second too late, either. I can see a box of sweet-and-sour chicken moving down there, and suddenly that fly ain't such a miracle anymore because I can see at least three more green-eyed flies bouncing around in the bag with their snouts dipping in and out of a month of our scraps. My grandpa used to say that tiny fish would appear in a mud puddle if it sits undisturbed long enough. Not true.

Those were mosquitoes. You know how they say the bathroom is the last place your girlfriend exists? I meant the garbage.

I take out the trash. Then I keep walking past the dumpster to throw my headphones into the river before I change my mind.

It's one of those rivers that looks good from a distance. Then you're standing next to it and you catch a smell of what's been dumped in there for years. Wasn't this the river that caught on fire because of the pollution? You'd think my toilet would have ignited from all the cigarettes she flicked in it. Is this the river where that little boy swore he saw the shark?

The headphones bob along, riding the brown waves, then something under the water takes a couple bites and finally pulls them down. There's a girl standing next to me when I turn around.

"You know what you looked like to me just then?" she asks. "You looked like the last scene of a movie. The part where the sheriff throws away his badge."

"Hold out your hand," I tell her, not expecting her to. When she uncurls her fingers for me, I expect something to fly away.

"What's your name?"

"Michelle. But I go by 'Chelle, 'shell.'"

"Of course you do. I've seen you before, haven't I?"

"I live in your building."

"Have you ever had problems with your wiring?"

"No," she laughs. "Have you?"

"All the time."

"You should get a surge protector. Seriously. I have three of them."

I stare for seven…eight…nine seconds. Then I write my phone number in her hand. Just for laughs I draw a fly underneath it. "Sorry, I like drawing flies."

"I know. They're easy to make. Like a smiley face. You know why everyone draws smiley faces? Because there are less than five lines you need before you can recognize it."

"I believe it."

I hear the buzzing sound again, and I know what it is before she even pulls it out. She smiles an apology and presses the phone deep into her face, quickly walking away before she starts talking.

I walk off in the opposite direction to give her some privacy. I think of my phone number and the fly I drew on her skin, and I cup my hand around my ear like a seashell. Even when she's miles away, even when her head and her hand are the only things visible above the waves smacking my head and filling my nostrils, I still keep my hand over my ear, and I can still hear every word of her conversation like she's swimming right next to me. Until I pull her under.

Remedy Blue

by D.N. Drake

HARLTON FLICKED HIS CIGARETTE AGAINST A BRICK wall as he walked out from the alley. A truck was being unloaded. It said *Remedy Blue* along its side.

Damn. It's been a good long month since my last drink.

He rounded the back of the truck and crossed the street. His tongue felt dry. It's not an option, he told himself. It's not an option. He recalled his girlfriend Georgia's face when she last caught him drinking a bottle of it. If you do it again, I'll leave you, she said. You choose what you love more.

His tongue wagged a bit between his teeth. I can almost taste it—a good Maine Spring on the rocks. He could feel it sloshing in his mouth.

The hot suns hammered down on him as his legs took him back to his post on the corner. He pulled the comedy club leaflets from his back pocket.

It was apparent to him that the day didn't want him to work. The heat was almost unbearable as it dripped down the tall glass buildings beneath the dusty red sky.

Harlton closed his eyes and recalled the cool blue Earth. He'd passed it en route to Mars once—one of his binge-filled visits to his Uncle Francis in the cervical mines beneath the gas brooders. Those biological mining machines extracted Banana gas (that damned replacement). None of the miners sniffed that shit, of course, they were too close to earth not to drink the sweet stuff.

Stop it. You're phasing back again. He held out his arm, his fingers loosely holding a crinkled leaflet. "You like comedy?" he asked a group of passing Japanese tourists—they pushed past him without even giving him a glance.

No? I didn't think you did, he thought, his face tightening at the jaw. How about a quick one then? Just a small glass. There's no way she would know. Harlton could feel two dollars in his back jean pocket. That could buy me a shot of Hudson River Estate and an ice cube.

The Remedy Blue truck pulled away and passed directly in front of him. He turned his head and his eyes stopped as they found the pub across the street—The Watering Hole.

The urge strangled him and constricted his breathing passage. Itches found spots up and down his legs and lower back. The heat smacked him in the face and smothered him.

C'mon! Aren't there ten billion people on earth still addicted to it? You think you're better than them?

A woman walked by inhaling a bottle of the yellow Banana gas into her nose. He looked at her and cringed. That stuff is so flippin dry and bitter—I can't be dealing with it.

Harlton let the handbills drop to the sidewalk in a flurry before hurrying across the intersection. He let himself forget about the mental shackles that water imposed on the human brain. He forgot about Georgia, he forgot about everything —everything except the cool water flowing down his throat. The fluid of the old world. The fluid that for so long held back the floodgates of true progress.

As he reached the other side of the street he instinctively pulled the money out from his pocket. A quick one, he said to himself. Just a quick sip.

He pushed through the doors, immediately feeling the cool and familiar humidity. He stepped up to the counter, "A shot of water and one ice cube please." He stuffed the two dollars in the bartender's hand.

After a quick look the bartender handed them back and laughed. "We can't accept comedy leaflets as payment, son."

Harlton felt his stomach fill up with gravel. He looked up from his handbills and found himself in the bar mirror opposite, the Remedy Blue logo silkscreened across his pot-marked face. You're worthless, he thought—and he licked up his tears as they came down over his lips.

AFFECTIONS BETWEEN SPACE

by JAMES BOONE DRYDEN

NAV-PILOT MARSHALL KNEW SOMETHING WAS wrong when he saw the emblazoned emblem of the Administration on the shuttle that was pulling into Yhon Station. He pushed the glass aside as he watched it dock through the large glass panes that looked out into the black space surrounding them. He turned in his chair to watch the whole process: the shuttle pulled slowly into the bay and settled gently onto the glossy platform; behind it, the nearly invisible airlock shield closed; then, the passenger hatch opened in the side of the shuttle—exactly where the emblem had been burned and painted into the façade of the ship—and two men walked down the small set of stairs.

Marshall tried unsuccessfully to identify them, but they were young—much younger than he—and he could only assume that they were rookie ambassadors sent on some errand to the far reaches. They passed through the air-locked doors that led into the station's main area, and Marshall watched them intently. They looked around for a few moments from the confines of the door's inset and then one of them motioned for a guard. There was a brief conversation before the guard turned, as did the two ambassadors, and pointed directly at the Pilot.

Marshall felt his heart jump. He turned, hoping that there was someone behind him or that the bartender had been the one that they were indicating, but there was no one else around him. He watched them approach and absently grabbed the glass that still sat on the counter next to him. He glanced down at the half-inch of liquid still in the bottom and raised it to his lips. With one gulp, he swallowed it and then coughed as his eyes watered.

"You are Nav-Pilot Peter Marshall?" one of the young men asked.

Marshall nodded.

"We have been sent to deliver a message to you of dire importance," the ambassador said. He paused. Marshall indicated with a nod that the man should continue. From rote, the ambassador announced quietly: "We regret to inform you that your wife, Alexandra Marshall, went missing three years ago and has since been located, though she was found deceased. It is the Administration's belief that she was victim to a homicide, and an investigation is currently underway as to her disappearance and death. The Administration sends its deepest condolences."

Marshall turned and looked for the bartender, but he was nowhere to be found.

"Alex is dead?"

"I am terribly sorry," the ambassador replied.

"According to the wishes stated in your writ of desires," the other ambassador offered, "she has been buried in New Haven alongside her mother."

"Thank you," Marshall said.

"It has been arranged that you may return with us," the first man said, "to attend a ceremony in her honor. Your ship will be quartered here at the expense of the Administration, and you will be given transportation back as soon as you wish to return. The Administrations understands that you might request some personal grievance time here at the station but asks that you take no more than two days to decide whether you will return or not."

"Does today count?" Marshall asked.

The two men turned and looked at one another, confused by the logic. There was a bit of quiet discussion between them before the first one spoke.

"No," he said. "We do not believe the Administration intended for us to arrive as early as we did. You have two days after this to make your decision."

"How kind of you," Marshall said.

He stood and gave the two men a terse bow. Then he slipped past them and made his way across the open-plan floor of the station towards his own ship. When he reached the recessed door to the bay that housed his ship, he stopped and looked over his shoulder. The ambassadors were both turned, looking directly at him. He wanted to turn and shout at them to mind their own business, but they were out of their element, and he was their only connection to this place. He pressed the button, and door opened. He stepped through and let the door close behind him.

Nav-Pilot Marcus Dietrich was Marshall's dock-mate. They'd worked out of Yhon Station for nearly ten years and had been assigned the same bay when they were given their Cruisers. Dietrich was a tall brute of a man that Marshall was hesitant to admit he knew little about. They drank together; they flew together. Once, they had even shared the same woman.

Marshall sat on the bottom step of his Cruiser with a glass in hand. Dietrich was quiet, walking purposefully around his ship for its weekly inspection.

"How long have they known," Dietrich asked.

"It took them nine days to get here," Marshall replied. "They knew where I was and how to get to me. No one ever told me that she went missing."

"Maybe she didn't go missing," Dietrich said.

"Maybe she found someone else," Marshall replied.

Dietrich turned to face Marshall and nodded.

"I don't understand why someone would kill her, though."

"Passion, maybe," Dietrich offered. "Did they say how she died?"

"No. They won't tell me anything about it."

"Perhaps something more sinister happened."

Marshall watched Dietrich as he worked. Perhaps something terrible had happened to her, and the Administration was too embarrassed or ashamed to tell him. There were things that they were hesitant to admit still happened in their well-guarded and over-protected world.

"I barely knew her, Dietrich."

"Then why did you marry her?"

"I thought I was going to stay," Marshall replied. "I thought that I would get a position nearby, so I could visit her often. I didn't think that they would send me here."

"You are respected and admired," Dietrich said.

"I wasn't then."

Dietrich didn't say anything. Marshall continued to watch him. He brought the rim of the glass to his lips, and the smell of the whiskey hit his nose. Marshall grimaced and looked down at the smoky brown liquid. He set the glass down on the polymer floor and kicked the glass away from him; it slid quietly across the bay and came to rest against the far wall with a quiet 'clink'.

"Have you ever loved someone?" Marshall asked.

Dietrich stopped his inspection and turned to look squarely at Marshall.

"If you didn't love her," he said, "it's ok to admit it."

"I did love her," Marshall said. "I just think that maybe I'd forgotten."

Dietrich seemed to think about it for a moment, then turned and resumed his inspection. After a while, Marshall stood and walked into his Cruiser and closed the hatch behind him. The whispered hiss of the airlock sealing behind him was comforting, and he relaxed a bit as he settled onto his bed.

"Good morning, Pilot Marshall," the ambassador said.

Marshall couldn't remember which one was which: they looked like they could have been clones—and knowing the Administration, there was no discounting that possibility.

"Hello," Marshall replied. He sat down at the table across from the man.

Yhon Station only had one eatery that could properly be called a diner. Outside of the vendors and hagglers that lined the circular center area of the Station, there was very little on the Station that was affordable to most Nav-Pilots or the Shuttlebums. Marshall had only eaten here once.

"I do not mean to pry," the ambassador said, "but I would be interested to know if you had made a decision yet."

"You mean the Administration wishes to know," Marshall said, "because the longer you're here, the more money they have to pay you."

The ambassador made a noise that Marshall took as a nervous chuckle.

"I have not yet," Marshall replied. "It may take some time, but I will make my decision by tomorrow."

"Of course," the ambassador said.

Marshall picked up the single sheet that served as the diner's menu and looked over the options. They'd changed things a little since that first time. Certain things were hard to get this far out, and Marshall imagined such a change was frequent and common.

"What would you like," the ambassador asked.

Marshall didn't question the ambassador's implication that he was going to be paying. There was never a time when a man passed up a free meal.

"I'll just take a sandwich," Marshall said.

The conversation between bites and gulps of fresh water was brief and stilted. Marshall didn't like the idea of his departure hanging over the table. He also didn't like the man's gaze as he watched Marshall eat.

When they were done, Marshall thanked the ambassador and left the diner. The station was quiet in the mornings, and Marshall was inwardly thankful for the solitude he was granted as he walked along the corridor that led from the diner to the central lobby.

It's strange to think that I knew so little of her. I can't even remember her birthday, but I know I sent presents. I can't remember her smell or how she felt. Does that mean that I've forgotten who she was or just who she is?

"Quiet and encompassing," Marshall said, "that's space."

"Your vision is much more optimistic than mine," Dietrich said. "I see it as cold, endless, and unwelcoming."

Marshall nodded.

"Have you ever loved someone, Dietrich?" Marshall asked.

Dietrich turned to look at Marshall and then turned back to gaze out of the invisible airlock shield.

"Have you still not made your decision?"

"I have," Marshall said. "You just never answered my question before."

There was a quiet moment, and Marshall thought that perhaps had over-stepped the unspoken rules of their relationship. Dietrich was a quiet man, and Marshall knew little of his past.

"I did once," he replied. "Unlike you, I came here to run from it, only to miss it even more. It is long past now, though, and there is no chance of reconciling."

Marshall nodded. Ten years was a long time to be away from

people you knew. It was an even longer time to be away from the people you loved.

"My father only wrote to me once," Marshall said. "I thought after that that he'd forgotten about me or couldn't bear the pain of not seeing me."

Dietrich turned and looked at Marshall.

"But after a while, I realized that people lose touch—not because they forget or hope to forget. Time begins to erase the present when you're so far away, and people lose touch because they can't feel you or see you or hear you, and they begin to use their senses on new people. But memories are what keep people alive in other people's minds."

"Did you ever write him back," Dietrich asked.

"Yesterday I did. He's been dead for six years now."

Dietrich turned again to look out at the stars and the empty space between them. Marshall sighed quietly and then closed his eyes to sleep on the bay floor.

The ambassador looked Marshall over with a pensive stare. Marshall did not say anything as the man gave him a look of what he read as disdain.

"You will not be coming," he said.

"There is no sense in it," Marshall said. "I am sorry to have wasted the Administration's time."

"It is of no consequence," the ambassador said.

"Will you take this back for me, though," Marshall asked.

He handed a sealed envelope to the ambassador along with a small, carefully-wrapped package.

"I need these to get to her father," Marshall said.

"Of course, Nav-Pilot," the ambassador said. "I will get them to her father."

The two young Administration men stepped through the dock door and made their way back to their shuttle. Marshall watched through the thick, clear plastic as they proceeded to board and prepare their ship. As it slowly backed out of the bay and into space, Marshall felt somebody slip up next to him.

"Do you think she had forgotten you," Dietrich asked.

"No," Marshall said. "I think she still loved who I was and who she married, but I'm not that person anymore, and I don't even know the woman that died. They could have been two entirely different people for all I know. I couldn't bring myself to try and conjure up some false emotion to show to her father."

"So what did you send him?"

"My wedding ring with a letter," Marshall replied.

Dietrich gave a quiet grunt.

"I had nothing else to offer," Marshall said.

My Salieri Complex

by MARINA JULIA NEARY

An Untold Story of Griffin and Kemp
(dedicated to H.G. Wells)

(University College, London, 1884)

"AWAKE, SAMUEL! BOARDING WITH A GENIUS WILL not tranform you into one."

That was the voice of reason, one that guided me through most of my career. Yet another voice, one of superstition and vanity, tried to persuade me of the opposite. How I wished to believe that a fraction of Jonathan Griffin's brilliance could project onto me if I only spent enough time in his vicinity! I fancied our brains being like two communicating vessels, with grandiose theories and mysteries passing between them. Little by little, that toxic swamp of self-flattering fantasies sucked me in.

Griffin, a native of Cardiff, was almost three years younger than me but only one year behind in his coursework. He transferred to University College in the autumn of 1883, allegedly to study medicine. I emphasize the word "allegedly." From the very beginning I had serious doubts that this man had any intention of treating patients for the rest of his life. As I learned later, medicine was the profession of his father's choice. Griffin feigned compliance only to gain access to London's best library and laboratory. He took most interest in optical density and refraction index, two topics that had very little to do with medicine.

We enrolled in the same physics seminar led by Professor Handley, my intellectual father, who promised me an assistant's position after my graduation, as well as the hand of his daughter Elizabeth. Everyone in the department regarded me as Professor Handley's heir, the future king of the laboratory. At least, that was the case until Griffin's arrival. In one week this eighteen-year old boy with a Welsh accent toppled the hierarchy that had been in place since my first solo demonstration in 1881. When Griffin would enter the lecture hall, all the chatter would cease and then turn into a collective sigh of veneration.

It happened so quickly that I did not even have enough time to grow suspicious, or indignant, or bitter. He snatched my invisible crown and placed it on his perfectly shaped head, atop a cloud of snow-white curls.

Griffin was the only albino I had ever encountered. At first he struck me as a member of an entirely different race, one that Darwin and Kingsley would declare as superior to their own, a race untainted by unnecessary pigment. Later I learned that the condition had its disadvantages. Griffin's eyes, garnet-red, were extremely sensitive to the light, obliging him to wear spectacles made of tinted glass and a hat. Between those eyes a permanent crease was forming, growing deeper by the month. I studied that crease furtively, as if it were some hieroglyph, a clue to the mysteries of his mind.

◊◊◊◊◊

As a child I suffered from respiratory distress. Slightest physical exertion caused me to pant and wheeze, cutting me off from the games of my sturdier peers. No, they did not taunt me. They simply refused to acknowledge my existence. At the time I would have preferred open ridicule to utter indifference. I found consolation in corresponding with Robert Louis Stevenson, who had also had a "weak chest" and spent much of his childhood in sickbed. He had shared with me the early drafts of his novels and poems. I read "The Treasure Island" long before it was published. His bewildering adventures distracted me from my affliction, provided me with an opportunity to step out of my treacherous, uncooperative body. By the age of sixteen I had reconciled with the thought that I would have no companions save for the merry crew of the schooner Hispaniola.

All that changed when I came to University College and discovered that in matters of intellect I surpassed most of my peers. Suddenly, my physical infirmities became inconsequential. A former outcast, I became the most sought-after individual in the entire medical department. My peers, who snubbed me during my adolescence, now fought for a chance to have me for a study partner. They rapped on the door of my flat, attempted subtle bribes, invited me to family outings. For once, I had the power of rejecting one companion in favor of another. I think back to the winter of 1881 and the succession of triumphs: my first public demonstration before the entire department, my first dinner at Professor Handley's house, my first evening with Elizabeth without a chaperone. Unnoticeably to myself, I outgrew my malady. This spontaneous recovery prompted me to make a vow to God that I would devote my life to treating the ailments of the lungs.

Then the white-haired Welshman barged into my kingdom, and my wheezing attacks returned, with doubled intensity. When I was near him, I lacked for air. Griffin was stealing oxygen from me. As slender as he was, as few personal possessions as he had, somehow he occupied most of the two-bedroom flat that we shared. Every corner bore the mark of his presence. Some elusive spirit reigned there, leaving very little space for me.

Griffin's bedroom served as his personal laboratory where he would continue his experiments into midnight. His dowry included an assortment of glass tubes in which he would heat and mix various chemicals. I knew better than to pry into the nature of Griffin's experiments, but I suspected it was the fumes seeping from under the closed door of his bedroom that triggered my coughing attacks.

Still, I had no grounds for complaints, as there was nothing criminal about Griffin's behavior. Who can fault a science student for diligence? If his work stirred my old illness, it was my private ordeal. Remains of pride forbade me to vocalize my growing discontent. Most of all I feared being accused of having a Salieri complex. There was nothing left for me to do except drive my anger deep into my inflamed chest. When the tightness in the lungs became unbearable, I would simply go outside or wander the corridors of the residence hall.

Nobody ever found out how many nights I spent on the cushions in the lounge. And nobody found out about the tempest inside my head. It was not my crown that I missed—it was my freedom. I learned what it meant to be a spiritual captive of another human being.

I knew that when my schoolmates knocked on our door, it was most likely for Griffin, not me. Rarely would he deign to come out of his sanctuary and greet them. Usually he would remain behind the closed door upon which our schoolmates would throw furtive, longing glances. With the immediacy of small children they would elbow each other and whisper.

"How long can he toy with explosives?"

"I know: he's making a bride for himself."

"No, he's building a time machine."

"Stop reading so much Jules Verne, dearest. It will do your pretty little head no good."

"At least I can read, unlike some of us."

"I tell you, albinos are all evil. It's a mark of the Devil."

"Listen to you! Sounding like you're straight from Oxford. Believing in the devil is no longer fashionable."

"Well, if the Devil exists, Griffin is his incarnation."

"Bah, you're just envious!"

"I say, he's dissecting rats."

"Bosh! One doesn't need to go to a university for that."

"This is no university. It's a glorified butchery."

"Gentlemen, is it just my imagination, or does Griffin's hair look a bit whiter than it was before? I didn't think it was possible. And his skin! Did you see his skin? It's translucent. You can see the veins and everything."

"Here's an idea. Why don't you knock on his door and ask him?"

"Like hell I will! You knock first."

"After you."

"No, after you!"

"Coward!"

"Idiot!"

Those were the typical conversations. Griffin this, Griffin that…

Yes, they still consulted me on academic matters. I convinced myself that they were doing it out of habit, or duty, or, perhaps, pity.

And yes, I was still welcome at Professor Handley's dinner table, but so was Griffin, although he did not take advantage of this privilege frequently. On those rare occasions when he joined us, Elizabeth would become noticeably distracted. She would study Griffin's face, as deliberately and as blatantly as her upbringing allowed, while he remained oblivious to her presence. He spoke very little and ate even less. Between courses he scribbled in his notebook, with which he never parted. His colorless lips kept moving, whispering formulas. His garnet eyes would squint and widen, as if from flashes of light. In those moments he resembled a monk immersed in perpetual prayer. And Elizabeth would sigh and smile sadly. Apparently, the white-haired genius struck a chord that I never had. Not that it mattered to me. One more defeat made no difference.

Handley, delighted to now have two adopted sons, nurtured his own designs. One Friday afternoon, towards the end of the seminar, he suggested before the whole group that Griffin and I should collaborate on a study.

Science professors cannot boast about being the most tactful men in the world. This is no earth-shattering revelation. Handley was no exception to the rule.

"Every semester my students grip each other by the throats for a chance to partner with Samuel Kemp," he said, beaming at his own ingenuity. "This time I decided to try a different approach. I will remove both Kemp and Griffin from the battle and assign them to each other. It would be presumptuous on my behalf to speak for the entire University College, but personally I am very anxious to see what miracles these two brilliant young men can concoct together."

For a few seconds everyone in the hall ceased breathing and looked at Griffin, for he, apparently, had the final say.

"Is this a mandate?" he inquired, tapping his lips with the tip of his pencil.

"Not at all," Handley reassured him hastily, "merely an unobtrusive proposal. Since you and Samuel Kemp already spend a considerable amount of time under the same roof, perhaps, you would use this time more constructively, for the benefit of your respective careers."

Griffin straightened out and clutched his notebook to his

chest.

"If this is a mere proposal, then I fear I must politely decline it, Professor. You see, I am not quite ready to share my work with anyone, even Samuel Kemp—with all due regard."

There was no deliberate hostility in his voice. Still, his declaration solicited a number of stifled gasps from the audience. What? The earth stopped spinning. Samuel Kemp received his first outward rejection! Now everyone was staring at me.

My chest tightened. I felt a sudden need to unbutton my collar. The prospect of having a coughing attack in front of my schoolmates petrified me. God be my witness, I tried not to be angry with Handley. Nor did I doubt his benevolence. The man sincerely believed his idea brilliant.

"Professor," I mumbled, raising a sweaty, trembling hand. "I was about to present the same objection, but Mr. Griffin preceded me. I believe it is in everyone's best interests that we work separately. Following his example, I will take no partner this semester. I would like to think that I have earned my autonomy."

Handley looked perplexed, not heartbroken.

"Who am I to argue with geniuses?"

He turned his back to us and began wiping the blackboard, letting everyone know that the class was dismissed.

◊◊◊◊◊

Several weeks went by. I remained faithful to my promise to work alone for the semester, spending my time in the mezzanine of the library, avoiding my schoolmates and Handley in particular. The date of my graduation was approaching, which meant I needed to start thinking about my impending marriage. Elizabeth had begun making wedding preparations, and I had no idea what that ceremony entailed. She had mentioned names of places, churches and reception halls, I had never heard of. In truth, my knowledge of London outside Bloomsbury was rather sketchy. I simply never had a reason to leave the cluster of buildings that comprised University College.

One Sunday evening, after the library had closed and I returned into my flat, something unthinkable happened. Griffin emerged from his laboratory and actually spoke to me.

"Samuel," he began with uncharacteristic softness.

I shuddered at the sound of his voice and pinched myself.

Griffin had never addressed me, let alone by my given name.

"I was made aware of the inconvenience I have caused you over the past few months," he continued. "I did not know until recently that my experiments were harming your health. You should've informed me at once. And then that horrid incident at the lecture hall! Handley took me by surprise. I suppose, I haven't grown accustomed to his antics. That buffoon of a man…"

I interrupted him quite coldly.

"You were about to say—"

Did Griffin truly believe it will take a few words of gossip to melt the ice?

"I was about to say that an apology would not be out of place."

"An apology?" I asked, shaking my head in confusion. "From me to you, I suppose?"

"Samuel, I would be honored to have you for a study partner. I was simply waiting for the appropriate moment to initiate you into my discoveries. I did not wish to do it before the entire class. Most of our schoolmates are sheep. But you know that already, don't you? Listen, I'm very glad that I met you, even in a place like this, amidst this bureaucratic circus."

I opened my mouth, but no words came out, only a hoarse wheeze. The glass tubes on the shelf began to blur.

"We have much to discuss, Samuel. It will take some time."

"Honestly, I'm flattered," I muttered, wiping the sweat off my cheeks and neck. "However, I meant what I said in the lecture hall. It isn't in our best interests to collaborate. You see plainly that I am in no state to argue with you. I simply don't have enough air in my lungs. Let us leave things as they are. Please, excuse me."

I turned around, preparing to leave, but Griffin, my idol, my tormentor, stepped towards me and caught me by the shoulders.

"I need one full night to work," he continued, as if he had not heard my objections. "Come back in the morning, and I will be ready to share my findings with you. This will be the last inconvenience to which you'll be subjected, one last favor. It will be worth your wait, Sam. I promise."

Losing footing, I leaned forward and buried my face on his chest, convinced that I was dying. The fumes from his shirt and his white hair were poisoning me. It was the first time we came into physical contact. Before then he had not as much as shaken my hand. Even on the verge of a swoon I could not help noticing how hot his skin was. Any other human being would be delirious at such body temperature. The protein in the blood begins to curdle at forty-two Celsius. It was one of the first facts I learned in my medical coursework. And Griffin's temperature must have been close to forty-five. But then, he was no ordinary human being. His body chemistry must have been different, either from birth or as result of mysterious manipulations on his part. And now this alien creature was embracing me, trying to cajole me into his plot.

Terrified and jubilant at the same time, I threw my arms around his neck and clung to him, coughing and laughing.

Suddenly, I heard him whisper.

"Collect yourself, Samuel."

It was neither a plea nor an attempt to comfort me but an order. Of course, he had no time for this.

Still panting, I released him. He escorted me to the door and, with a slap on the back, pushed me into the dark hall.

"Good night, Samuel."

◊◊◊◊◊

When I came to my senses, I was walking down Gower Street, where every stone in the pavement was familiar to me. Over the last few months I had learned the pattern of the cobblestone. Those clusters of ovals and lopsided rectangles had turned into a mosaic of bewilderment and muffled fury. But that night I felt strange heat radiating from those stones, like the heat from Jonathan's hands. Those stones were alive. They whispered to me, as I was still trying to make sense of the sudden reversal of fate.

He and I…How blind, how inattentive we both had been!

I must confess that the promise of partnership and camaraderie with Jonathan thrilled me more than my engagement to Elizabeth. Her acceptance of my proposal held no triumph for me. I never pursued her aggressively, and she never resisted. One evening Professor Handley, as unceremonious a matchmaker as he was a peacemaker, simply seated us side by side at the dinner table. It was a marriage of reverence that we shared for her father. When we said 'yes,' it was not so much to each other but to Professor Handley.

Elizabeth was sturdy and well-mannered, though not remarkably beautiful, not in the same sense that Jonathan was. Before meeting him, I had never regarded other human beings as beautiful or ugly. My aesthetic sensibilities awakened fairly late. Suddenly, I discovered the desire to look at another face, marveling at the clean, elongated lines of the profile and the exquisite translucency of skin. It struck me as strange that the elation, the source of which should have been Elizabeth, was instead sparked by Jonathan. Strange, but not in any way wrong.

◊◊◊◊◊

In the morning, when I stopped by our flat to change my shirt and fetch my textbooks, I found Jonathan's room empty. I assumed I would meet him in the lecture hall. I could not help wondering how we would behave in front of our schoolmates. Would we publicize our newly formed friendship? Perhaps, he would prefer to keep it a secret and then stun the entire department at the end of the semester.

I have witnessed, on more than one occasion, scenes of jubilation when study partners, after receiving an award for a successful demonstration, would hang on each other's necks, skip, squeal like pups and kiss each other "on the brain" as the called it. Then they would rip off their ties and give each other back rides up and down the hall, to the applause of their mates. It was a chance for these future high priests of science to temporarily turn into savages. Thankfully, they did not practice such boorish antics with me, knowing my distaste for them. Perhaps, I had a stricter upbringing. Undoubtedly, even the most civilized men need a release, especially if it is well-earned. Still, I could not fathom embracing Jonathan by the shoulders in public, no matter how much I wanted to.

When I entered the lecture hall, I saw Handley's assistant. The professor himself was absent. So was Griffin.

When the assistant saw me, he pulled me aside.

"Mr. Kemp, Professor Handley wishes to see you in his office."

The request to see the professor in private did not disturb me. I could not recall doing anything that would lead to repercussions. I assumed that the nature of the conversation would be purely academic. Perhaps, Griffin informed Handley about our decision to collaborate and requested some funds from the department.

With a fairly light heart, I came into Handley's office. He was there in the company of another professor by the name Ellsworth.

"Please, sit down," Handley commanded, pointing at a vacant armchair. "I am afraid I have some disturbing news. Your flat mate Griffin was taken to the infirmary earlier this morning, in a very grave condition."

"God help him," I mumbled, sitting down on the edge of the chair. "What happened?"

"Nobody knows for certain. He won't talk to the doctor. He exhibits every symptom of severe poisoning: vomiting, pallor, listlessness, reduced circulation in the limbs."

"Well, can I see him?"

"Not yet. The doctors insist on keeping him secluded."

"Why on earth?"

Here Ellsworth intruded.

"Samuel, do you know why we called you here?"

"Because I am Jonathan's friend, naturally."

"How odd," Ellsworth commented, rubbing his chin. "I did not think that Jonathan had any friends. But he certainly had his share of enviers. The doctors have reasons to believe that what he is suffering from is no ordinary infection. There is evidence of highly toxic substance in his bloodstream. The director is contemplating bringing in the constable, who may wish to question those with whom Griffin has had contact. We wanted to prepare you for this possibility. You may be among the first ones to be interrogated."

Had I had any strength left in my legs, I would have leaped up from the chair. All I could do was press my fingers into the wooden arms.

"Don't fear, Samuel, we aren't trying to incriminate you," Handley chimed in hastily. "On the contrary, we are trying to protect you."

"I know what made Griffin ill," I blurted out, staring into the floor. "He drank one of his concoctions."

The professors shook their heads in tandem.

"You aren't implying that it was a suicide attempt, are you?" asked Ellsworth.

"Nothing of the sort! It was an experiment."

"An experiment?"

"Yes! The substance he took was supposed to destroy the pigment in his blood without altering its properties. I've heard him mumble formulas in his sleep. Pigments, optical density, refraction index, transparency of living tissues, radiation machine…"

The professors assumed the same pose—arms crossed, heads tilted. As I continued, Handley's eyebrow kept arching steeper and steeper.

"So, what was the objective of his experiments?" he inquired. "In your opinion, what was Griffin trying to accomplish?"

Handley's dimwittedness infuriated me indescribably. How long would it take him to assemble the pieces of the puzzle?

"Gentlemen," I said, struggling to keep my voice steady, "is it not obvious that Griffin's goal was to turn invisible?"

Both professors burst out laughing. Handley was so amused that he needed to pour himself a glass of water from the carafe on his desk.

"Scientific impossibility aside," he resumed after the first sip, "why would a young man endowed with Griffin's appearance wish to make himself invisible? I couldn't help noticing the effect he has on the fair sex."

"Griffin doesn't care about women!" I exclaimed. "You don't understand. He doesn't care about anyone, least of all himself. He will risk his life for his work. I've grown to know Griffin like no other. You can laugh at me now to your hearts' content. You didn't stand behind the closed door of his bedroom for hours, listening to him rant in his sleep. Please, let me see him. I can persuade him to let the doctors treat him. He'll listen to me. We can save him. I've been thinking of little less for the past four months."

My eyes must have been tearing, because Handley offered me his handkerchief. Ellsworth leaned over to his colleague and mumbled loudly enough for me to hear.

"Something tells me that this is no longer a story of Mozart and Salieri. Rather, it is a story of Byron and Shelley."

Handley, who was not very versed in romantic literature, did not understand the allusion at once. He began chewing on his lower lip as he usually did to mask his ignorance.

"This would be far worse for the school's reputation," Ellsworth continued hissing in his ear. "Sensitive young men, when deprived of female companionship for prolonged stretches of time, can fall into all sorts of unwholesome, unnatural affections towards each other. Don't you know? In ancient Sparta…"

The more Ellsworth spoke, the more perplexed Handley grew. History was another subject outside of his expertise. Both carried on as if I were not present.

"Of what crime exactly am I being accused?" I asked at last, glancing up. "Let us be clear. Is it attempted murder or homosexuality?"

Now that was a word that Handley understood. His jaw dropped, and his hand grasped his tie as if it were choking him.

"Young man! Have you no shame?"

"Shame? Shouldn't you be posing this question to your colleague? A student is dying, and Professor Ellsworth revels in the most piquant practices of ancient Spartans. Apparently, that is where his mind dwells. Those night walks that he took down Gower Street with the drama professor must've led to Sparta. But who am I to judge? After all, this is a secular, liberal university, a cradle of progress. Still, all you care about is your precious reputation. It comes before everything, even science. And then you wonder why students hide from you."

Handley threw a plaintive glance at his colleague.

"My weak heart won't take it. I'm getting much too old for such an ordeal. What is happening to our institution? And above all, why is this happening on my watch? Two of my best students…After everything I've done for them! I gave Samuel a seat at my dinner table and my beautiful daughter in marriage. And this is his gratitude I receive!"

"Right before the end of the semester, too!" Ellsworth replied sympathetically.

"Let me see Griffin," I demanded through my teeth. "I don't care whom you drag into this. I will stand before the entire Scotland Yard if necessary. I have nothing to hide, and I don't need anyone's protection."

Handley pulled his tie off his neck and wrapped it around his fist.

"Go," he muttered half-audibly, swinging the silk ribbon towards the door.

◊◊◊◊◊

The drowsy nurse on duty barely stirred as I entered the chilly hall of the infirmary. All curtains were closed tight at Griffin's request, who was the only patient there that day. For a minute I lingered at his bedside, studying the outline of his scrawny body under the white sheet. He did not acknowledge my visit in any way, even though he was wide awake. His eyes were fixed on the ceiling, and his hands were still clutching his notebook.

A malicious thought flashed through my head. This was my opportunity to exact revenge, however superficial. I could threaten to expose his failed experiment to our schoolmates, to make him the laughing stock of the entire University College.

But that moment of gloating lasted only a second. I reminded myself that I was a doctor in training and, as such, took the liberty of feeling his forehead. Now, it was not much warmer to the touch than the metal bedpost. I estimated that his body temperature was barely hovering above thirty degrees.

Judging from the hue of his skin, his experiment was not a complete failure. He looked even paler than before, which led me to conclude that he succeeded at destroying some of the pigment in his red blood cells.

"What a shame, Samuel," he began, still staring upward.

His voice was surprisingly strong, given his wretched condition. He did not look defeated in the least.

"I had every intention of initiating you into my work," he continued, "but you simply can't keep your mouth shut."

"Neither can you," I retaliated, sitting down on the edge of his bed. "You ought to consider gagging yourself for the night."

"How much did you hear?"

"Enough to confirm my theory that you were not here to study medicine."

"I wish I could," he lamented. "Sometimes I wish I could take interest in something as mundane as medicine and practice it for the rest of my life. I wish I could be content with Handley for a professor and his homely daughter for a wife. But I'll never be like the others. I always suspected it, but when I came here, all doubt was removed. This is no place to practice science."

His head twitched on the pillow, and his gaze shifted to me. This sudden attempt to make eye contact threw me into a state of slight panic. I came close to jumping up from his bed. His icy hand released the notebook and seized my wrist.

"I must leave at once," he declared.

"Perhaps, it would be for the better," I muttered faintly. "No need to stay in a place where you feel stifled."

For an instant I thought that he was going to ask me to abandon everything and follow him, to the end of the world, wherever he was going. I don't know what made me think he would propose such a thing.

He released my wrist as suddenly as he seized it.

"By the way, you need not fear," I continued. "Nobody will find out."

"Oh, yes, they certainly will find out," Griffin objected. "The whole world will—in due time. And those rotten hogs from the academia who scoffed at me will tremble. The whole world will tremble."

The whole world! Griffin despised it enough to want to hide himself from it, yet at the same time he coveted it enough to want to dominate it.

"Will I ever see you again?" I asked.

"Not if everything goes according to my plan. I'll be sure to visit you when my work is complete. You won't see me, but you'll hear my voice and feel my grip."

He arched his back on the mattress and laughed.

"Jonathan, you'll kill yourself!" I said, rising to my feet and backing away from his bed.

"Don't let your hopes soar."

◊◊◊◊◊

Five days later Griffin left the university, citing poor health in his exit letter. One afternoon I returned from the lectures and found the flat cleared of his possessions except for one cracked tube that he left behind and which I kept it as a souvenir.

Once again, I could spend the nights under my roof without the fear of suffocating. Once again, I was the king of the laboratory. Not that it mattered anymore. My schoolmates began flocking back to me, their demeanor being apologetic, almost servile. I did not respond to their insinuations. Their voices blended into one indistinct buzz. The only voice I heard distinctly was that of my former flat mate. Jonathan succeeded at infecting me with his contempt for the University College. I began viewing that place with his eyes and feeling stifled there. Once my coronation site, it suddenly became my prison. Graduation could not come soon enough. I did complete my solo demonstration and even received an award which left me completely indifferent.

Needless to say, I never accepted the teaching position that Professor Handley had promised to me. Nor did I end up marrying Elizabeth. It was difficult to say which one of us was more relieved to break the engagement.

Stevenson continued writing to me, sending drafts of his stories and poems, but I never responded.

I felt that by continuing to love my respectable, philistine life that Jonathan despised so, I would somehow betray him. Perhaps, if I proved myself worthy and denounced all things ordinary, he would return to me and share his secrets at last. Those sentiments were completely absurd and ludicrous. I owed Griffin nothing. No man should have such power over another.

When nobody was watching, I would pinch, slap and shake myself, trying to break free from that bizarre vision of Jonathan, the white-haired, garnet-eyed angel dissolving into air.

FINISHERS OF MEN

by DON NORUM

CLAIRE WOKE UP EARLY, BEFORE THE COMMUNAL alarm went off, and climbed down the ladder past Alice and Tomoko. In the bathroom stall, door wedged against her back, she rubbed her skin with a lukewarm sponge before dressing. At her foot locker, she removed her pocket Bible and turned to the back to gaze at the photo-collage of her patron saints. Kasczynski. Dahmer. Bum-kon and Toi. As Alice stirred in the middle bunk, Claire returned her icons to their places and bade her roommates good morning before joining the rushing tide outside of their door.

◊◊◊◊◊

It had been a cancer cure, originally—some sort of gene therapy retroviral. Ironic, in a way—of the two great bugaboos of late-modern medicine, one had been turned on the other. A modified form of the HIV-6 virus had been able to repair the cellular damage, the genetic aberration. Reverse transcriptases were the new blue jeans and p53 tumor suppressor the new black.

◊◊◊◊◊

The Chinese kid who ladled her tray at the cafeteria at breakfast shift three had a lapel plate reading "Smile! Today is the first day of the rest of your life!" Claire ground her teeth and cleaned her plate.

"You like poetry?"

She looked up and saw a man peering at her from across the table, black hair tucked back underneath a brimmed cap. He sat with a cafeteria mug of tea and a battered personal reader.

"Some."

"Ever read George Jay Harris?"

"Can't say that I have," she said.

"Oh, he's great. Optimistic, uplifting, all that jazz." The man slid the reader across the Formica and tapped the top of the screen. "Check it out."

Claire gave a grimacing smile as she evaded jostling elbows on either side to take the slate and read the block of text displayed in the center.

Don't speak to me of shortage. My world is vast
And has more than enough—far more than enough.
There is a shortage of nothing, save will and wisdom;
And there is a longage of time.
— *GJH*

She pulled a pencil out of her pocket and twirled it in her fingers, tapping the eraser against the screen now and then as she mused on the poem. After a minute, she handed it back to the man.

"Can't say that I've ever read that, but it's decent. He write anything else?"

The man took the slate back and looked at the screen before tapping away the poem, which now read

Don't speak to me of shortage. My world is vast
And has more than enough—for no more than enough.
There is a shortage of nothing, save will and wisdom;
But there is a longage of people.
— *GJH*

He slid his finger around, calling up files and volumes.

"Well, if you're interested in his earlier pastorals, there's his 'Southern Meditations', then he's got 'Songs of My Fathers,' 'The Joys of Company,' oh, bunches. Have you got a reader with you? I could share you a couple of copies right now."

Claire pursed her lips and shook her head.

"No, I'm off to my shift right now—damn, a few minutes late, in fact—and I left my reader at home. I'll just have to remember the name."

The man looked hurt, but then gave a wide shucksing grin.

"Tell you what, here." He held out his hand and produced a memory card. "I've got a few books on here I take with me to work, to read over break. I work in the aqueducts right now," he added, "so I'm not too keen on having my personal reader short out from all the moisture."

Claire shrugged and took the card from him, tucking it into her breast pocket.

"Thanks. I'll give him a look this evening. How should I get it back to you?"

He waved her off.

"Don't worry about it. Used to be the best gift I could give anyone was a good book, and this is as close to that as I can get now. Keep it—enjoy."

The man drained his mug and smiled at her as he stood up, turning and leaving. He set the mug on one of the busing conveyors and was lost in the crowd leaving the room.

The news-crawl on the widescreen in the corner announced that a myoclostridium spore contamination of the Angelino arcology had resulted in the deaths of one hundred and twenty seven. The Pope came on, the captions in Latin blackletter proclaiming a mass of unraveling, and Claire left to catch the lift up and out to the farms.

◊◊◊◊◊

The recombinant virus that Doctor Morgan had brewed up went into clinical trials after three years—tests had to be done to insure that it wouldn't create the disease it was based off of. First trial groups consisted of middle-stage pancreatic adenocarcinoma patients with fully developed AIDS. They chose those with different strains from the modified virus so that they could test to see if it replicated in the body. Tests of body fluids proved negative—the virus was staying in the tumors.

◊◊◊◊◊

Claire slipped into a bunny suit, greeted Tami Viswanathan, and stepped out onto the vertical-film floor. The farm spokes extended from the core of Tower Four on each level, making the New York arcology appear as a series of interlocking gears when seen by the weather satellites.

She set to work slipping seedlings from sprout trays into the slots on the hanging sheets. A conveyor track carried the vegetables from the interior of the spoke, where nutrient mists coated them, back to the outer rim where pure sunlight shone down. The farms fed the towers a subsistence diet, supplemented by the few fields to the south.

"You need anything from Central?" Claire asked Tami.

"No, thanks," she shook her head. "What's up?"

Claire raised a gloved hand, holding a transparent sprout-pouch with a wrinkled green shoot inside it.

"Spot check on the gene line. My number's up."

Tami sighed in sympathy. The arcologists ate only a handful of different plants, cloned a million times over for maximum yield and efficiency. Quality control measures like this were necessary to prevent genetic plagues.

Claire sealed the pouch in a sterile container and checked out of the film-floor. It was a short walk back to the center of the tower after changing out of her bunny suit, and she spent the minutes poring over a report on a small reader.

The card from her breast pocket had clued her in that today would be her day to carry a specimen of Arachis Ahmedna to the central repository, where the various gene lines were prepared and shipped out to the culturing spokes below. The engineered variety of peanut named after its creator was allergen free and easier to process than the wild type.

As she came to the entrance to the repository, she tucked the reader into her pocket and held up the sample case to the intern at the scanner. He ran a laser over the coded static square and glanced at the computer.

"Looks good, Ms. Whitenack. Go on in—I'll let them know you're here."

Claire walked through the door and looked around the neat laboratory. Benches and free-standing tables divided the room into long strips, glass tubes and metal boxes of genetic analyzers covering their tops. A woman in a white coat walked down one of the rows and greeted Claire.

"Is this the A. Ahmedna from Spoke 8-H?"

"Yeah. Haven't had any problems with this strain for years."

The woman nodded and smiled.

"You can never be too careful, though."

"True, true," Claire agreed. "How are things going?"

"Going just heavenly," the scientist replied.

Claire signed out to return to the film floor as the scientist left to compare the genetic material of the sample with the master strain stored in the spoke's storage cells. Each tower had its own varieties, varying from one another just enough to avoid turning a collapse into a catastrophe. Before she left, though, she availed herself of a high temperature incinerator chute for laboratory waste, tossing down the reader and a small plastic pouch with a green shoot in it.

After reading the message from the man in the cafeteria on her way to the lifts, she had made a slight detour to meet another woman in a bathroom and get from her an identical pouch containing a shoot, identical in every way save one to the A. Ahmedna sample she just burned.

The Vehements had obtained a recombinant sample of the allergen-positive peanut genome three months ago, by her estimation, and it had taken that long to modify it to pass the genetic tests and then to find a way to smuggle it into the arcology's food supply. There were too many filters and safeguards once the foods left the farms to contaminate them there, so they had to go to the source.

By now the scientist would have compared the two samples and logged the results into the computers. The genetic tests would show that the two samples matched – the allergen operons had been moved to a different locus, one that wasn't compared to the A. Ahmedna reference —and from there it would be a simple matter to swap in the new code for the old.

She went back through the decontamination procedures, put her suit back on, and went back to the monotonous task of opening up the small pouches and inserting them into the film sheets that rotated like full-length tie racks around the edges of the spoke.

◊◊◊◊◊

The treatment had gone into widespread use soon after. Tumors stopped growing and were gradually absorbed in over half of the cases. No operation was needed, just a microscopic injection. Doctor Evelyn Morgan became the youngest—and fastest-awarded—Nobel laureate in Medicine. Full workups were still being done, but the sheer scale of the success just this once outweighed the concerns of rigor. Patients with months to live saw Christmas roll on into New Year's and back to Thanksgiving. Brain cancer patients with seven weeks to live were alive seven years after treatments.

◊◊◊◊◊

Claire and the rest of the workers broke at midday for a brief meal and announcements and then resumed work. She had three months left in this job before she would be rotated out to the algae farms. The only people who stayed in a career were the scientists or the open-land ranchers—and the latter were the last of the Dying Breeds. At the end of her twelve-hour shift she took the crowded lift back to the Block Three common area and checked out a reader to pass the time until bed, as she had every day for the last twenty years.

The new strain introduced into the arcology's food supply would take some time to be propagated and spread to the whole tower. When that happened, one percent of the population would be vulnerable. If they were lucky, they would manage to kill a tenth of that, and that was assuming the allergens would contaminate the workings they came into contact with, the hysteria would increase accident rates, and so on.

Politicians continued to debate the issue of overpopulation, but their attempts at addressing the problem were feeble and ineffectual. Individuals who opted for voluntary sterilization were hailed as the solution to the problem when a hundred babies were born in the time it took them to undergo the procedure.

She logged off of the reader and returned it to the desk, walking back to her room to go to bed. It was a necessary evil, and the imperative element of it was its necessity. A hundred years ago they had preached the same message, but back then —even among its disciples—the circumstances hadn't justified the message's implementation, only the underlying theory.

◊◊◊◊◊

When the cancer patients had survived for seventeen years, a miracle was announced. When they kept on living, when their health stayed robust in areas far removed from cancer, suspicions arose. But by then it was too late. When they first found evidence of the systemic retroviral action throughout the whole body, the mutated virus was already spread wild through the population.

◊◊◊◊◊

On the widescreen, a news-crawl interrupted the Pope's Humanae Vitae Redux address to announce that a Vehement terrorist had been apprehended trying to slip Biopreparat Marburg into the livestock processing in Chicago-III. The Pope reaffirmed Mother Church's opposition to any and all forms of birth control. Claire lay in bed staring at the ceiling as her roommates filed in behind her.

The genetic repair of the Morgan virus had extended to the telomeres. Biological clocks were stopped in their mid-thirties. Children began needing hormonal boosters to trigger puberty, but by the time the true effects became clear, they had been building for fifty years.

The New York arcologies were at fifty million each. UN predictions of ten billion had been laughed at ten billion births ago. Breeder reactors were built, and the arcologies sprouted around them like abyssal worms to a vent. Of all the world's cities, only New Londinium and Paris had put cessation hormones into the reservoirs before it was too late.

As Claire slept, she dreamed of sterilizing reactor malfunctions, of raging epidemics, of a freedom from the chains of the mass of humanity. Morgan had killed herself a hundred years ago and in that had at last redeemed herself. None of her fellow Vehements were suicidal—they were merely despairing, aiming for extinction, and hoping against hope that in failing to climb to that lofty goal, they would find themselves falling short into a better world.

As the now-never-ending tide of humanity pulled down the lofty aspirations of civilization one by one to replace all of it with the coarse business of brute survival, she prayed, prayed that the dread god Malthus would release humanity from its self-imposed prison to a future worth living for.

O HOLY NIGHT

by PAUL LORELLO

THE LAST PULSE OCCURRED IN 5642, THE ONE before that in 5632, the one before that in 5622, and so on. But each Pulse had come a minute or so earlier than the last, and one was left with the inevitable conclusion that they were increasing in frequency. We knew with the surety of atomic decay that the time would come when, at least for a while, they could be enjoyed annually. That is, until the frequency increased on the order of once every ten days, then once every ten seconds—and what would happen when they reached that undefinable pitch? For now though, it was enough that they occurred once every ten years.

The occasion of the most recent Pulse was savored with great delight among the younger folks, who possessed a near-limitless quantity of nerve in the face of such a great unknown. Most of these kids are too young to remember the insurgence of the ungodly black Slicks, who may seem tame now that they've all found their own tranquility wrapped in thick striation around and up the trunks of the nation's conifers (came the now-famous line "How about bark? Does anyone here remember the color of bark?" which was most likely never uttered at all) but were hellish on their arrival, oily and eyeless. And most of the kids do not remember, although their parents and their grandparents retell it with rising alarm in their voices, the tremendous outpouring of chunky red sand that came bubbling in great gobs out of the Pulse—and that had to be carted in teeming truckloads to the top of Mount Aura. There's a reminder of the occasion every winter when the summit burns bloody just before the onset of twilight.

And certainly none of them know the name Dr. Albert Difkind, although their horsehair strands—intercranial carbon nanotubing to you and I—could probably have the information in mind faster than you or I could look it up the old way. But ever since Difkind centralized the location of the Pulse using nothing more than a couple of Casimir plates, a light gas gun, and an ampule of pure sodium, kids gather at the Difkind spot on the night of the twenty-fourth and they wait. Sometimes they join hands and sing. Sometimes they sing without joining hands. Sometimes they tell crude jokes which they follow with crude laughter. Their method of enjoyment has changed, but the enjoyment itself is timeless. And even those who come away bruised and scratched have a happy and wonderful time.

But the real joy is in the weeks before, when the excited anticipation of whatever may arrive via the next Pulse is enough to start the heart pumping hurried hot blood through the extremities. Some of the older ones say that the time should not be rushed. That the days and weeks preceding the Pulse should be a time of reflection and quiet servitude to the senses. That the time before is merely time to suppress anxiety, for that is what strengthens the spirit. But try telling that to the hordes of kids whose behavior changes in the same way that dawn changes night into day—wholly, pervasively through the atmosphere. The Pulse cannot come soon enough for them. And I say let them be. They don't want their parents watching them anyway. If we stay far enough away, we can enjoy it with them. But I doubt we can enjoy it as much as they do, with aeons of life ahead of them, aeons of Pulses refreshing their world over and over again.

Dr. Difkind said there would one day be a way to keep track of the ever-changing origin of the Pulse. This footnote in his research was quickly forgotten (I don't need to tell you it was forgotten on purpose, do I?), but there is a movement—a small one, but a movement nonetheless—to resurrect Difkind's methods so that we may prepare ourselves more rigorously for whatever may arrive.

But I say, as my children do, that imagination is the only thing that is to be prepared rigorously, and that is all.

And so the time finally came after many dark weeks breathing frozen, smoky air. It culminated in a feverous, bustling last week of hurried meetings—as if the people greeting each other had only seconds to do so and would link up with them via horsehair at some later time—perhaps after the Pulse but not now, for heaven's sake, not now, we'll see you after the Pulse.

After the Pulse. There would be an after. That there had been so many afters since the first Pulse was cause for much joy.

And so my children went to the Difkind spot and joined the rest of the folks who stood around all wrapped up in layers like fat pastries. And as they waited, wind-blown, red-cheeked yet hot in their clothes, some of them sang, and the song caught on the way the tops of trees catch on to the song of a gale.

And the Pulse came.

As it had in the past, it started with a point. A dot of something in the few micrometers of space between the two metal plates. As the plates automatically collapsed on the instant amid a suppressed cheer, the dot swelled into a sphere until it reached the Difkind radius.

And what was to come through, came through.

An influx of briny-smelling things with many segmented legs, each rippling body the size and color of a walnut. Within minutes, a smell like a stray dog steeped in pickle juice pervaded the entire area. The crowd moved like a receding tide to allow them entrance into our world.

Some of the things expired quickly. Somewhere on our planet was a place capable of sustaining them, which is why the Pulse chose Earth over anywhere else. They would find that place soon. But it was necessary for the weaker ones to die off quickly due to their inability to adapt. Better for their future and ours. Some people in the crowd wept for them. Some of the more adventurous bared their arms and touched the frozen ground, inviting the surviving ones to scuttle up and nestle flat against steaming skin.

A few stayed and broke out in song. The rest dispersed and left the skittering things to find their way in the cold. That was the Pulse that year.

We welcomed our boy and girl back into the warmth and comfort of home, and after they'd unwrapped themselves they came to us. And we held them as they shook with sobs, and we didn't think of letting go.

The next night they downloaded some stuff about the ancient rites of Christmas. It was hard not having a horsehair strand to connect with them. And it was harder to consider the fact that some of the information might have been kept in mind and not shared aloud. But they told us some things about it. And we sipped our chocolate and laughed and cried around a ceremonial conifer, its trunk smooth and striped with oily black.

AUTHOR BIOGRAPHIES

Sanford Allen (*Burma Jukebox*) has worked as a newspaper reporter, a college journalism instructor, and a touring musician. He recently released his first novel, *Deadly Passage*, and his short fiction has appeared in numerous magazines and anthologies.

A lot of writers have great ambitions. Some of them want to change the world. Some want to touch people's lives. Some want to achieve immortality. Some want to make boat loads of cash. **Brian Anglin** (*Einstein Rode Bitch*) is not one of those writers. Brian Anglin writes because it makes him popular at cocktail parties, and being a writer dramatically increases his chances of picking up chicks. So, if you would like to invite Mr. Anglin to attend your cocktail party, you can send your request to Brown Bag Publishing. If you would like to read his works, you can find them in small, genre magazines throughout the country, obscure websites, and on Amazon.

Adam Armour (*Mike (My Second Roommate)*) is an award-winning writer and photographer for a small newspaper in Mississippi. He is married, has three cats, one dog, and single kid. He is double-jointed in both arms, although he realizes this is not indicative of the actual number of joints. He has a scar above his upper lip, which he received after falling on his face while chasing a wiener dog down his grandmother's driveway. He has written one book, *Strange Beasts in a Small Town*, which didn't do all that well. Yap with him on Twitter @admarmr.

Keyan Bowes (*Lepers*) is a graduate of the Clarion Writers Workshop, a life-changing experience. With two dozen stories and poems published, Keyan's work has appeared in *Cabinet des Fees*, *Expanded Horizons*, *Big Pulp*, and *Strange Horizons* among others, as well as in a dozen anthologies. Her story in this collection was first published online at *Big Pulp*, and has since appeared in a German publication. "Chick Lit" has been translated into

Polish; "Nor Yet Feed the Swine," published in *Cabinet des Fees*, won a sought-after "Recommended" review from *Locus Online* reviewer, Lois Tilton. "The Rumpelstiltskin Retellings," a story in poetry-blog format, was made into an award-winning short film, "Rumpled." Keyan is currently rewriting two Young Adult novels in the contemporary fantasy adventure genre, and working on three short stories. Visit her online at keyanbowes.org.

Although **Michael Bracken (*Dead Things*)** is the author of several books, including the private eye novel *All White Girls*, the two-time Derringer Award-winning writer is better known as the author of more than 1,100 short stories published in *Alfred Hitchcock's Mystery Magazine*, *Crime Square*, *Ellery Queen's Mystery Magazine*, *Espionage Magazine*, *Fifty Shades of Grey Fedora*, *Flesh & Blood: Guilty as Sin*, *Mike Shayne Mystery Magazine*, *Weird Menace*, and in many other anthologies and periodicals. Learn more at www.CrimeFictionWriter.com and CrimeFictionWriter.blogspot.com.

Tim Deal (*The Deep End*) is a writer and former publisher living in New Hampshire. He travels the globe trying to make the world a safer place. His fiction has appeared in several magazines and anthologies.

Thomas Canfield (*Riding to Hounds*) aspires to worry less, for which purpose he has taken up the study of children, and to laugh more, for which purpose he has taken up the study of politicians.

Tom Conoboy (*Skin Like Shining Armour*) has a Master's degree in creative writing and a PhD on the fiction of Cormac McCarthy. He has been published in a variety of print and e-journals and anthologies and has recently completed his first novel.

D.N. Drake (*Remedy Blue*) has been published in *PostScripts SF*, *Southern Fried Weirdness*, the *6S* ezine, and *Foliate Oak Literary Magazine*. He is also the editor of the sf ezine *The Courier*, and submissions editor for the award winning magazine *Abyss & Apex*.

James Boone Dryden (*Affections Between Space*) is a graduate student pursuing a joint JD/MFA degree at Hamline University in Minnesota. He has previously been published on *EveryDayFiction.com*, *365Tomorrows.com*, *Big Pulp*, and in *Left of the Lake Magazine.*

Cathy C. Hall (*Mary Beth's Prophecy*) gets around in both kidlit and adult markets. You'll find her byline in the *Uncle John's Bathroom Reader* series, *Puppet Plays for Libraries*, The *Atlanta Journal Constitution*, and plenty of *Chicken Soup for the Soul* books. And if you happen to be in Korea, look for her children's titles from Darakwon Publishing. She's like the *Where's Waldo* of the writing world, only way better dressed.

J.A. Kazimer (*Honey, Is That a Dead Hooker Under the Bed?*) lives in Denver, CO. When she isn't looking for a place to hide the bodies, she spends her time with a pup named Killer. Other hobbies include murdering houseplants. She spent a few years as a bartender and then wasted another few years stalking people while working as a private investigator before transitioning to the moniker of WRITER. Visit her website at jakazimer.com. Connect with her on Twitter (@ jakazimer) and Facebook (/JulieAKazimer).

David James Keaton's (*Sharks With Thumbs*) fiction has appeared in over 50 publications. His first collection, *FISH BITES COP! Stories to Bash Authorities* (Comet Press), was named the 2013 Short Story Collection of the Year by *This Is Horror.* His second collection of short fiction, *Stealing Propeller Hats from the Dead* (PMMP), recently received a Starred Review by *Publishers Weekly.* He teaches composition at Santa Clara University in California.

Paul Lorello (*O Holy Night*) is a freelance writer from Ronkonkoma, NY. His fiction has appeared Big Pulp's anthologies *The Kennedy Curse*, *Black Chaos*, and *Way Out West.* His writing also has appeared in *Membrane* and *Pseudopod.* In 2014, the *Pseudopod* podcast of Paul's story, "Growth Spurt", won the Parsec Award for Best Speculative Fiction Story, Short Form. Paul also has a story forthcoming on the *Glittership* podcast.

Kristin McHenry (*Spock: A Romance in Quotes*) is a resident of Seattle, WA, where she is a poet by night, manager of hospital volunteers by day. She has her bachelor's degree in theatre arts and filmmaking from The Evergreen State College. Among other publications, her work has been seen in *Bare Root Review*, *Numinous Magazine*, *Tiferet Journal*, *Sybil's Garage*, *Big Pulp*, and the anthology, *Many Trails to the Summit*, published by Rose Alley Press. Her chapbook *The Goatfish Alphabet* was runner-up in qarrtsiluni's 2009 chapbook contest, and was published by Naissance Press. Another chapbook, *Triplicity: Poems In Threes*, was published by Indigo Ink Press. Kristen serves on the editorial staff for Literary Bohemian, and teaches creativity workshops in her "spare" time.

David Melody lives in the Columbia Gorge region of Washington State. "For Sale" is from a series he is working on titled Snap Shots He has had stories in *GHOTI* and *The Writer's Eye Magazine.*

Kristine Ong Muslim is the author of seven books of fiction and poetry, including, most recently the short story collections *Age of Blight* (Unnamed Press, 2016) and *Butterfly Dream* (Snuggly Books, 2016). She grew up and continues to live in rural southern Philippines.

A self-centered, only child of classical musicians, **Marina Julia Neary** (*My Salieri Complex*) spent her early years in Eastern Europe and came to the US at the age of thirteen. Her literary career revolves around depicting military and social disasters, from the Charge of the Light Brigade, to the Irish Famine, to the Easter Rising in Dublin, to the nuclear explosion in Chernobyl some thirty miles away from her home town. Notorious for her abrasive personality and politically incorrect views that make her a *persona non grata* in most polite circles, Neary explores human suffering through the prism of dark humor, believing that tragedy and comedy go hand in hand.

Don Norum (*Finishers of Men*) writes things. Sometimes they are published.

Terrie Leigh Relf (*On the Many Uses of Duct Tape for Resolving Relationship Issues*) is a writer. editor, and certified life coach living in the eclectic community of Ocean Beach. You may learn more about her by visiting tlrelf.wordpress.com and terrieleighrelf.com.

Jason S. Ridler (*Melancholy Dust*) is a writer and historian. He is the author of *A Triumph for Sakura*, *Blood and Sawdust*, the Spar Battersea thrillers, the short story collection *Knockouts*, and has published over sixty stories in such magazines and anthologies as *The Big Click*, *Beneath Ceaseless Skies*, *Out of the Gutter*, numerous *Big Pulp* publications, and more. His popular non-fiction has appeared in *Clarkesworld*, *Dark Scribe*, and the *Internet Review of Science Fiction*. A former punk rock musician and cemetery groundskeeper, Mr. Ridler holds a Ph.D. in War Studies from the Royal Military College of Canada.

Match Ryan (*When Molly the Necrophiliac Went on a Date With Suicide Stanley*) holds the MFA in Writing from Spalding University. His fiction has been published in *Word Riot*, *elimae*, *Pequin*, *Yellow Mama*, *Bewildering Stories*, *Clockwise Cat*, *Boston Literary Magazine*, and *Writers Notes*. He is an editor for *Best New Writing* and a professor of English at Concordia University St. Paul.

Wayne Scheer (*Doing God's Work*) fiction has appeared numerous times in *Big Pulp*, most recently in our Spring 2013 and Summer 2012 issues, and in *Thirst*.

Shannon Schuren (*Psychic Karma*) lives in Sheboygan Falls, Wisconsin. She works as a librarian and finds spending her days surrounded by books both inspiring and intimidating. Her short stories have appeared in *Toasted Cheese Literary Journal*, *Vine Leaves Literary Journal*, *Big Pulp*, and *Ellery Queen Mystery Magazine*. Her short story "Puddings" was awarded the top prize in prose poetry in the Eighth Annual Binnacle Ultra-Short Competition and was also nominated for a Pushcart Prize.

Erik Secker (*Erik Secker*) published a small magazine in the 90s that featured original fiction by many award-winning writers. He lives in Austin, Texas, with his wife and two kids.

Helen Silverstein (*It Might As Well Be Me*) has been published in *Big Pulp* and *34th Parallel Magazine.*

Anna Sykora (*A Burning Question*) has been an attorney in NYC and teacher of English in Germany, where she resides with her patient husband and three enormous cats. To date she has placed 142 stories, mostly genre, in the small press, and one made the finals of Rosebud's 2014 Mary Shelley Competition. She has also placed 420 poems. Writing is her joy.

LaShawn Wanak (*Lavender and Chamomile*) writes speculative fiction and blogs at The Café in the Woods (tbonecafe.wordpress.com).

www.ingramcontent.com/pod-product-compliance
Lightning Source LLC
Chambersburg PA
CBHW051254250626
47155CB00009B/3290

* 9 7 8 0 9 8 9 6 8 1 2 4 7 *